THE VICTIM
A beautiful married woman. She needs to be noticed, to be loved. What she gets is murdered.

HER PSYCHIATRIST
Someone quite disturbed is leaving messages on his phone machine. Someone who has his straight razor.

HER SON
He's got evidence that can finish the killer. And the killer's got a blade that can finish *him*.

THE CALL GIRL
A suspect, desperate to clear herself, she's walking into more danger than she can handle.

DRESSED TO KILL

SAMUEL Z. ARKOFF
Presents

A GEORGE LITTO PRODUCTION
OF A BRIAN DE PALMA FILM

MICHAEL CAINE
ANGIE DICKINSON
In

DRESSED TO KILL

CO-STARRING
NANCY ALLEN

WRITTEN BY BRIAN DE PALMA

PRODUCED BY GEORGE LITTO

DIRECTED BY BRIAN DE PALMA

DRESSED TO KILL

A Novel by
Brian De Palma
and
Campbell Black

DRESSED TO KILL
A Bantam Book/July 1980

ISBN 0-553-12977-5

Published simultaneously in the United States and Canada

PRINTED IN THE UNITED STATES OF AMERICA

0 9 8 7 6 5 4 3 2 1

ONE

1

She had passed the place a hundred times before tonight, watching those who went inside, watching them as they moved beneath the discreet neon and through the doors—and sometimes, when the doors swung back briefly, she could hear the noise of music. It had something to do with the music, she thought. Something to do with how it seemed to emerge in broken phrases like a series of quick invitations. *Come in. It's the easiest thing in the world. Just come in.* She turned away and crossed the narrow street. On the sidewalk opposite she paused, put her fingers up to the edges of her dark glasses, shivered. But it wasn't cold. Nerves. Maybe it came down to that failure of nerve in the end, something that simply snapped and left you suspended in a vacuum. She raised a hand to the strand of blonde hair that had fallen across her forehead, and she wondered how she looked, if she looked good enough to compete in a place like that.

Compete. What kind of thinking was that? She didn't have to compete with anybody. She had only to cross the street and push the doors back and she would be inside—but the thought paralyzed her. Now she saw a man go through the doors. She saw how the neon was reflected off his thinning hair. Don't be nervous, she told herself. Go back across the street. Go inside. Follow the music. She looked at her image in the darkened window of a shuttered drugstore. The dark glasses almost obscured her face. Dark glasses at night: maybe that was pretentious. And the short fur jacket seemed to emphasize her height, making her feel awkward, ungainly. She pushed the strand of hair away once more.

You fought nerves with nerves, she thought. You

didn't just yield to fear. You turned it around so that it was something positive, not this negative energy.

She put her hands inside the pockets of the jacket. She shrugged so that the purse slung around her shoulder wouldn't slip. Then she turned away from her own reflection and moved slowly back across the street. Nothing to fear, she thought. You go through those doors like anybody else. She closed her eyes a moment under the neon. *Somebody might come and try to pick you up, and you might be attracted, and you might want to spend the night with the man, you might want the sweet careless moment of anonymous fucking in a dark room. . . .*

She shivered again, realizing now that she'd gone through the doors, that the music was louder, the room lit only by a series of dim shaded lamps, as if you might come and go with the stealth of a shadow. She moved towards the bar. She thought: Sharks. A room of dark sharks shifting through the shallows of light. The barman was leaning towards her, saying something. She couldn't hear. He repeated his words. And then her mind was empty, she couldn't think what to say, couldn't think of anything she wanted to drink, conscious only of sensations—the music that sounded like the crying of rooks, the smell of sweat and deodorant hanging around her, the weight of her purse against her shoulder.

"Let me," somebody said. "If you don't mind."

She stared at the face of the man who had spoken. A fleshy face, middle-aged, with the kind of expression you associated with people who had stood too long in a line, waiting for a ticket or to make a complaint in a department store. She could feel herself smile. The man moved closer to her. *Peppermint.* The smell enveloped her. She sighed, trying to relax.

"What'll it be?" he asked.

She gazed at him. There was something flat in the accent, something that suggested the great emptiness of the plains and prairies; it didn't have the hard nasal quality of the city. His hand fell on her wrist.

"Scotch. On the rocks," she said. But her voice seemed faint, coming from a great distance. The drink was poured and pushed across the surface of the bar towards her, then the man was helping her on to a stool, the palm of his hand covering her elbow.

"Walter," the man said. "Walter Pidgeon."

"Eva," she answered. "Eva Braun."

The man laughed. "I'm serious. That's my real name. Nobody ever believes it."

She watched him a moment. Walter Pidgeon from the Midwest. Maybe in a bar like this everybody had a pseudonym. Maybe they came armed with the artillery of false identities. Fear of reprisal. Plain old fear.

"If you're not Eva, who are you?" he said. He was drawing a stool towards her, then climbing up on it. He leaned close to her. She could feel his arm against her own. She said nothing for a moment. She sipped some of the scotch. Then she turned to face him. There was something soft and forlorn in his features, a loneliness, a suffering.

"Bobbi," she said.

"Bobbi." He appeared to suck on the word, like a lozenge whose flavor he wasn't sure he liked.

"With an i," she said.

"Bobbi," he said again. "Do you have a second name?"

"Sometimes." She finished the drink, put the empty glass down, and looked around the room. It was funny how all the fears had dispelled themselves now; it was weird to think how terrified she'd been. Through the dim lights she could make out the shapes of groups of men, girls, standing around looking confident, almost arrogant; and she could feel a certain conspiratorial quality about the place, like everybody knew they had come here to try to score. To score, she thought. A sporting metaphor. The game of fucking. The gladiatorial arena of a singles bar.

"Is that your second name?" Walter asked. "Sometimes?"

She smiled, turning back to look at him. Bobbi Sometimes. Then something moved inside her head, a shadow, a flicker of darkness, a thing she couldn't put a name to. *Bobbi Sometimes*. She stopped smiling, feeling the rise of a tiny panic inside herself. Maybe he wasn't making a joke, after all. Maybe he had seen through her. Like one of those laboratory slides you hold up to the light. A pinned butterfly. A blood specimen. *Seen through her.* What was she thinking? There wasn't anything to see through. There wasn't anything at all.

"Another drink?" he said.

She nodded, looking down at the empty glass. She heard him call the bartender. Then she felt his hand close around her knee and she let it lie there for a time before she pushed it gently aside. Walter laughed.

"Moving too fast," he said. "Impulsive. Can't help it. It's in my blood."

She raised her second glass and said, "Where do you come from, Walter?"

"Small place you probably never heard of," he said. "Pocatello, Idaho."

"You're right. I never heard of it." She looked at him over the rim of her glass now, conscious of the fact she was flirting vaguely with him, flirting in a way that was almost halfhearted. "What brings you to the big city?"

"Convention," the man said. "But you don't want to talk about that. Sugar beets don't make for interesting conversation, honey."

Honey, she thought. She felt warm suddenly. The drinks. The sound of the word *honey*, the way he said it, as if it were a solitary word that had strayed from the lyric of some song. Honey honey. She felt his hand close around her knee again.

"Why don't you take off the glasses?" he said.

"I like them—"

"I want to see your eyes. I bet they're blue."

She shook her head. "I like the glasses," she said again. "They make me feel . . ."

"Secure?" Walter said.

"Secure, right."

Walter bumped against her. The drink in her hand shook. She felt a spot of spilled liquid seep through the material of her pants. But it didn't matter. She shut her eyes and listened to the music. Soft rock. Gordon Lightfoot. *Sundown, you better take care . . .* She lowered her hand so that it covered Walter's. She moved her head a little from side to side, feeling her hair against the sides of her face. A cocoon. A place where you could withdraw. A whole little world of make believe. *Somehow you've known this man for years, you've been lovers for a long time, you're the little number he keeps in the city, where his wife doesn't know, you're the very first person he calls when he arrives, the person you've been waiting for, aching for. . . .*

"I'm at The Americana," he was saying.

His words, his voice—why did they intrude like that?

"Room six-oh-nine."

She didn't want to open her eyes. The song held her. The touch of hands. *I can see you lying there in your satin dress. . . .* She thought: Say honey to me again. Call me that. Say it to me one more time.

"You want to leave here?" he asked.

She opened her eyes. The real world. The room of predators.

"We could have drinks in my room," he was saying.

She put her glass down. She shook her head.

"Why not?" he said. "We could have some drinks sent up. We'd have some fun."

She shook her head a second time. "I've got someplace else to go."

"Another date? Something like that?" Walter took his hand away from her knee. She felt exposed when he did so, vulnerable, as if she'd been betrayed somehow.

"Something like that," she answered.

"Lookit, you could call, you could say you've got this bad headache, make an excuse. . . ."

She stared at him. The music stopped. There was a strange silence in the bar. She imagined every conversation coming to a halt at exactly the same time, words slithering over precipices into silence. She felt unnerved. The Americana. Room six-oh-nine.

"I can't," she said.

"You don't find me as attractive as I find you, that it?"

She smiled. *He finds me attractive.* Me! She looked down at her empty glass. "It's not that," she said.

"This other appointment—a guy?"

"Right," she said.

Walter sighed. He rolled his eyes in exaggerated frustration. "Tomorrow night, honey, I catch a plane back to Idaho. I don't know when I'll be back again. I don't know if I'll *ever* be back."

She hitched her purse up over her shoulder. I want to go with you to your hotel, Walter, I want to ride with you in the elevator, go to your room, have those drinks, have that thing you call fun, I want to fuck you with the lamps turned off and the TV playing silently, I want all these things. . . .

"I can't," she said. Dear God, I can't. And she felt a sudden surging of an old anger, a rage the color of scarlet, as if she could see her own blood course through her body. And she was sucked into the wild stream of it, sucked and drawn along, a prisoner in her own arteries, choking on the mad tide of herself. I can't, I can't. . . .

"It's not just a one-nighter," he was saying. He looked pathetic, pleading. "I like you. Soon's you came through that door, I liked you. I don't go in for one-night stands, honey. It's not my style."

She looked into the palms of her upturned hands, thinking how large the hands seemed, how clumsy— unmade for the intricate delicacies of love. She got down from the stool and moved towards the door. I shouldn't have come in here, she thought. Walter was hurrying along behind her. She passed through the door. She heard him call to her. She stopped. She turned to face him. He placed his hands on her shoulders and she saw his face come close, closer, his lips slightly parted, as if with one last kiss he might convince her to stay with him. She felt darkness press in on her. The kiss was hot and damp. His hand went inside her fur jacket, the palm fumbling for her breasts. She closed her eyes and let the kiss take her over, a peppermint kiss, and she thought again of his hotel room and what it might be like to have him inside her, giving herself like that, a total yielding, all the goddamn barriers broken down at last—then she pulled herself away, chilled, horrified, turning aside from him.

"Hey, what's the matter?" he said.

But she wasn't listening, she was walking quickly away from him, then running, hearing her name called along the sidewalk. *Bobbi. Bobbi!* She turned a corner. The heel of her shoe broke, snapped, and she limped hurriedly, trying to catch her breath, her shoulder purse slipping, her ankle all at once sore. She came to a diner, the only place lit on a dark block. She went inside and sat at a table away from the window and ordered coffee when a waitress came. Her hands were shaking when she lit a cigarette. Goddamn. How could she have?

Try and relax, Bobbi.

Take it easy now. Breath deep, breath slow.

There was a lipstick mark on the rim of her coffee cup. Trembling, she turned the cup to the other side and drank the tasteless liquid. A telephone, she thought. There had to be a phone in this dump. She looked around. A chef in a greasy apron was wiping a hot plate, talking to the waitress as he did so, conversing in a language that didn't make any sense—Italian? Turkish? She didn't know. She got up from the table and went inside the lady's rest room. The smell of urine was sickening. On top of the trashcan there was a discarded tampon, crumpled, bloodied. She gazed at it for a moment, then looked at her face in the cracked mirror, trying to see . . . See what? A cubicle door opened, a woman lurched out, staggered past her, went back inside the restaurant.

Calm now, Bobbi.

Put the panic away. The anger.

But the anger was harder somehow.

The anger was harder to fight against.

She took a tube of lipstick from her purse, leaned towards the mirror, made her lips into a funnel, and brushed some color across them. She'd got it wrong. Smeared it. A clown could look like that. She grabbed a tissue and wiped her mouth. She opened the restroom door and went back inside the diner and walked to a telephone located in the corner near the door. She fumbled some coins out of her purse, stuck them in the slot, dialled the number.

He wasn't there. But then she'd known he wouldn't be, not at this time of night. Shrinks didn't work late. An answering machine with the sound of his voice. The noise of the beep irritated her.

Fight it, Bobbi. Fight the anger.

This is Dr. Elliott. I am out of my office at the moment. When you hear the sound of the beep, leave

*your name and message and a number where you can be
reached. Thank you.*

Damn him. She hated that cold English voice, the
precise way he spoke, like he couldn't stand the feel of
words in his mouth. She gripped the receiver hard.

"Elliott. This is Bobbi. Remember me?"

She paused. Maybe it wasn't a machine. Maybe Elliott
was really listening.

"I've got a new shrink now, Elliott. I don't need you. I
don't fucking need *you*. He's going to help me. He knows
how to help me. Not like you. He's called Levy. Maybe
you've heard of him?"

She stopped. She stared across the diner. The chef was
looking at her, grinning like a dumb jerk. A stupid empty
expression.

"But we're not through yet, Elliott. I'm not finished
with you yet. . . ." She twisted the cord round her wrist,
cradled the receiver between ear and shoulder. "I took
something from your office today, Elliott. Guess what?
Can't you guess, Doctor big shot shrink? Look in your
bathroom. Maybe you'll get warm. Maybe. I'm not going
to give you any more clues." She paused, then she whis-
pered, "Fuck you." And she put the receiver down hard.

She returned to her table and drank the rest of her
coffee. She tried to imagine Elliott listening to the taped
message, then searching his bathroom, looking, not knowing what he was looking for. It was funny. She slipped her
hand inside her purse, rummaging through the Kleenexes,
the battered cigarette packs, the items of cosmetics, until
she found the smooth surface.

Smooth, a worn wooden handle. Steel encased in wood.
The hard, clean, cold steel of an old-fashioned open razor.
She shut her purse.

2

It was a dream, the same dream, and even as it happened
Kate knew it to be a dream—at first frightening, then
pleasurable, then painful at the end because she knew she
would open her eyes and find herself in bed with Mike
and nothing would be different; sunlight would be burning
through the bedroom windows, motes of dust floating like

disintegrating moths, and Mike would reach across the
bed for her and make love in his perfunctory way, as if
each stroke of sex were a form of calisthenics, aspects of
some ritual exercise.

She didn't open her eyes. She thought about the dream.
She thought about it before it finally eluded her, before
it faded into a dark alcove of her mind. The stranger in
the dream ... who was he? The man in the shower stall
... where had he come from? And why couldn't she rid
herself of the odd feeling that his touch, although rough,
was somehow familiar to her? But then lots of things in
dreams were familiar in a distorted way. You went inside
rooms you knew by heart, and you recognized them, but
they were altogether different even if you couldn't say
how. Dream rooms. Dream landscapes.

Dream lovers.

She tried to bring the dream back, forcing her mind to
the memory.

*She steps into the shower. She sees Mike through the
frosted glass of the shower door. She turns on the water.
Mike sings to himself tunelessly as he shaves. The same
tune, always the same damn tune.*

And then there was a blank moment. Something happened after that. What happened next? What was the
exact order of events?

*A hand is clamped across her mouth as the water
streams over her. A man's hand. She feels his breath
upon the back of her neck. She feels his arms wrapped
tightly around her body from behind. She wants to cry
out. She wants to shout Mike's name. Mike goes on
shaving, distorted through the frosted glass. The air is
thick with steam. Condensation runs down the glass. Mike
shaves, sings. She can't scream. She can't move. And then
everything is turned upside down and she can feel this
man, this stranger, enter her from behind, and the pain
is terrible. But the pain only lasts for a second and then
she finds herself slowly parting her legs, still trying to
call out to Mike, still trying to wrench the iron hand away
from her mouth.*

It changed then. It changed the way dreams do.

*She feels him thrust upwards and she raises herself
higher, parting her legs wider, and after that she isn't*

*trying to call out Mike's name any more, Mike doesn't
exist except as some surreal imprint on frosted glass, the
only real thing is the feeling between her legs, the sensation of waves beginning to churn inside her, warm waves
moving at some deep inner level, and how she tries to
open her legs wider still, the muscles in her thighs and
calves trembling and aching, but the pain isn't pain any
more. It's like she doesn't exist now, like some part of her
has gone, then the water isn't falling any more, and Mike
isn't singing, and she's caught up in some profound
silence of pleasure, caught in a place where noise isn't
necessary, where there's only the quiet savagery of feeling.*

And she comes. In the dream, taken from behind by a
figment of her own imagination, she comes, and when she
does the silence is shattered by the echo of her own
screaming; the silence is stained glass broken into a mosa-
ic beyond any conceivable pattern.

And then the dream finished.

She opened her eyes. Coming up from sleep was like
slowly floating up from the depths of dark water. But it
was only a dream, nothing more. And if the touch of the
stranger was familiar, shit, that didn't mean anything
except you'd dreamed him before. Other worlds, she
thought. Maybe that was it—like some kind of astral
travel bullshit. Dimension hopping. Nightly, the same
other-worldly lover awaits.

She tried to push the bedsheet aside, but Mike was
watching her.

She turned to look at him. He was saying something
about how restless she'd been, how much she'd turned
and tossed in her sleep. Then he put his arm over her
naked breasts. She moved closer to him and tried to
imagine herself back in the dream. She tried to imagine
Mike as the phantom stranger. Phantom stranger, she
thought. For Christ's sake. (Elliott would have something
to say about this dream. He'd stick it in some neat
Freudian box and hand it back to her with ribbons on.
He'd drag out those labels so essential to his trade—guilt,
anxiety, repression. Damn, those terms were as necessary
to Elliott as Tru-Lanol Arterial Fluid and Lyf-Lyk Tint
were to an embalmer.) She shut her eyes. She felt Mike's

mouth 'against her own and she thought: He hasn't learned how to please, how to make it gentle, lasting, how to make it seem that it really mattered. He climbs on, climbs off, as if I was a blowup doll you could order from Frederick's mail-order catalogue. (*I'm Kate, five foot three, and I'm built to please.*) She listened to his rhythmic breathing, the steady beat of his stomach against her own. She moaned, twisting and arching her body as he began to come. I should get an Oscar, she thought. I'm expert at making him think he's good. Sweating, Mike slumped against her, stroking her hair lightly with one hand. It was the Tender Moment. It lasted, on average, fifteen seconds; then he'd get up and go inside the bathroom. And she would feel sore between her legs because he'd bruised her.

She watched him rise now, saw the fixed smile on his face, watched him vanish beyond the bathroom door; then there was the sound of running water. She lay with her hands clenched, the cold sheet drawn up across her body. She didn't feel angry, sad, upset—only a strange numbness that she understood was connected with the dream in a way she didn't fully grasp; it was as if she'd left part of herself behind, drawn a dark curtain upon the scene in the shower. Bullshit, she thought. You can't live in dreams. She threw the sheets aside and stepped out of bed, pulling on her robe, running her fingers through her messy hair.

Mike came out of the bathroom, a towel wrapped around his waist. He was still smiling, like a craftsman proud of something he'd just hammered together.

"What time are we meeting for lunch?" he asked.

Lunch. She'd almost forgotten lunch. She looked at herself in the dressing table mirror, picking up a brush now, running it haphazardly through her fair hair.

"One," she said.

"Don't forget," Mike said.

"I won't." She considered the lunch. A goddamn ordeal, sitting down to eat with Mike and his mother; that frosty face, with its inbuilt expression of suspicion, peering at her across the breadsticks and the wineglasses. Not that *she* ever drank, the old bat; but she made it clear, with her cold eyes pressed into narrow fleshy slits, that she disapproved of alcohol almost as much as she disapproved of her son's marriage to Kate. *I never believed my son would marry a widow,* she'd said once. *It's rather like trespassing on a grave, don't you think?* A widow, Kate thought. It was a weird label, as if you were possessed from beyond the grave. As if you were still the bride of the dead. But that thought hurt, it hurt with more pain than she wanted to carry, so she shoved it aside the way the good Doctor Elliott had told her to. (*Look, you don't need to carry grief around. It's excess baggage. If you think of your emotions as suitcases you want to take on an airplane, then you're going to get charged extra for grief.*) He was good with those sayings, Doctor Elliott. He had a finely tuned ear for the comforting platitude.

"Promise," Mike said. "You know how she likes punctuality."

"I know," Kate said. She turned from the mirror to face her husband. *There.* She caught herself doing it again, making the impossible effort to superimpose the face of Thomas on Mike, but it was like a blurred Polaroid picture, it was like something snapped by a hapless photographer who'd forgotten to turn to the next shot. Thomas is dead, she thought. Thomas had the bad fortune to step on a land mine in a far country and Thomas is therefore dead. Jesus Christ, could she never put that away? Could she never stick that one in some attic of her awareness and forget?

She felt sad again.

She said, "Girl Scout's honor. One o'clock. Sharp. I'll be there."

"Good girl," Mike said.

She watched him as he began to dress. Then she went to the window and looked down into the street. It was one of those quiet streets that, surrounded by the rabble of New York traffic, by the whines of ambulances and the screaming of cop cars and the honking of taxicabs, takes you by surprise—as if you'd stepped into another country altogether. She watched a yellow cab cruise below. Across the way a uniformed doorman, stepping out from under a dark red canopy, called to the cab. A woman cradling a small dog emerged from the apartment building and, holding the dog in a manner that suggested a mother with

a newborn child, stepped inside the taxi. Kate dropped
the curtain from between her fingers.

She turned to watch Mike dressing.

He fastened his cuff links. "Will Peter be joining us?"
he said.

Peter, she thought. She considered the line of battle
between her son and his stepfather, a no-man's-land
where the possibility of a truce, of amnesty, seemed not
to exist. Maybe that was all perfectly natural. Peter be-
longed to a dead father; nothing could change that. Peter's affections lay buried in Thomas's grave. And Mike
had all the finesse of the proverbial bull in the china shop
when it came to relationships with kids, especially a kid
like Peter.

She sighed. "I guess so," she said.

"Make sure he wears something except for those god-
awful combat jackets," Mike said. "They make him look
like a refugee or something."

"I'll try," Kate said.

"The way that kid dresses . . ." Mike let his voice fade.
She knew the rest of the sentence anyhow; he had repeated it until it had the feel of a catechism. *Slovenly.
Like some junior hippy, for God's sake.* She watched her
husband for a moment and she thought: It can't be easy
for him either. The shoes of a dead man. A sense of being
stalked by a ghost, a specter he saw reflected in Peter's
eyes. The resentment in the boy's face. (*How could you
marry again? How the hell could you do that? I don't
understand!* Peter, with watery eyes, hands clenched,
breath coming fast, accusing her of treachery . . .)

She saw Mike go out of the bedroom, then she could
hear him in the kitchen. She could hear him fill the
coffeepot and, in her mind's eye, picture him fastidiously
spooning out the required amounts of that coffee he
drank—what was it? French Market? Bitter and black
and tasting of chicory or something. She glanced at her
face in the mirror. Lines. Weariness. She shook her head
from side to side. And then the dream came back to her
in a flash of strange clarity, brief and quick and bright like
a bulb popping. She felt the water running over her and
the firm grip of the hand over her mouth and the man's
hardness between her legs and she thought: It's sad when

a dream is more real than the world around you. It's so goddamn sad.

She turned away from her own reflection. Sometimes you saw more than you needed, more than you wanted. Like just then—a hunger in the eyes, a hunger for a return to the dream.

Outside the door of Peter's room she hesitated. She thought of the alien world that lay inside. Peter's world, self-sustaining, self-perpetuating, hermetic. A world of gadgets, of experiments in various stages—wires trailing out of boxes whose purpose she couldn't even begin to guess, batteries, scraps of paper covered with his feverish handwriting, the strange hieroglyphics of whatever he was pursuing; a world of radios stripped down, electronic toys disembowelled, printed circuitry scattered in a haphazard way across the table, strewn over the floor, over his unmade bed. *A fucking little Einstein,* Mike had said when they'd once argued over the kid. *One day I'll plug the coffeepot into the wall and—wham! Frazzle City. You'll see.* She put her hand on the doorknob, still hesitant to go inside. A mess, a great mother of a mess; and yet there was a curious sense of order about the room, as if the chaos had been planned meticulously, as if the boy had followed a blueprint of disorder.

She knocked lightly, then she went inside.

He was sitting at his worktable. In one hand he was holding a smoking soldering iron, in the other a printed circuit board, a jumble of skeletal lines that meant nothing to her. He didn't look up, didn't even seem to be aware of her standing in the doorway. She stared at his black hair, unruly, ruffled, and the way his spectacles gleamed in the sunlight that came through the window. Suddenly it seemed to her that he was a replica of Thomas: the angle of the head, the lips pursed in concentration, the brow lined. A fifteen-year-old replica of a dead man. She felt a dry thickness in her throat, a pulse beating faintly in her skull like some dying bird's wing. A dizziness, a feeling she'd known before when she saw Peter in a certain light from a certain angle.

We buried Thomas just before the snows came, she thought. On a day the color of slate. We buried him just as the frigid dark of winter was covering everything. Another Vietnam statistic. One of the late ones ... She remembered a blur of things suddenly, the terrible telegram, the feeling of a scream locked up in her heart, the way she'd held Peter as if nothing were more precious to her now than the dead man's son. It came back, it came back like a black flood. She held the side of the door, waiting for the dizziness to ebb away from her. Eight fucking years, she thought. A widow with a seven-year-old son. Eight miserable fucking years ago. The lonely empty nights when the hunger was dreadful and all she could think about was the flesh decaying in the ground, and she'd understood the way to madness lay in that direction, that she was making a descent into the crazy inferno of her own macabre imagination. Dreams. Dreams of Thomas putting his foot down on a land mine. Dreams of explosions, the sky filled with rage, with the redness of blood, the tendrils of torn flesh.

She shut her eyes for a moment. It would pass, she knew. Once, she would have gone for the Valium or the Equanil or whatever salve Elliott might think fit to prescribe—but now she'd learned to control it without chemicals. It would pass. All you had to do was hold on.

Peter looked up at her. "I didn't see you come in," he said.

There were small dark circles under his eyes. She said, "You've been up all night, haven't you?"

He nodded. "I've got to get this thing finished. The science exhibit is next week."

"I know. You keep telling me that. As an excuse, kid, it's pretty threadbare." But she couldn't bring herself to scold him; she lacked the cutting edge in her voice. And he knew it, because he was grinning at her. "What's your secret, Peter? You ever sleep? I mean, like us common folks, you ever settle your head on a pillow and kinda close your eyes and just drift off into the land of nod, huh?"

She stood over him now, putting her hands on his shoulders, massaging him very gently. He said, "Who needs sleep? I read someplace we spend about one third of our life in bed. Can you imagine that? I mean, one third of a whole lifetime *spent in bed?* It's a waste of time."

She smiled down at him. "What's that you're doing anyhow? Cracking an atom or something?"

"It's a microprocessor," he said. "You wouldn't really understand."

She was amused at the way he sometimes patronized her. What the hell, he was right. She wouldn't know a microprocessor from an acorn. She stared at the printed circuitry, then at the tangle of things on his table. Insane, like a mad scientist.

"Suppose, egghead, you explain to me." She folded her arms under her breasts and stood in the manner of somebody who has been waiting years for an explanation.

"I couldn't," he said. "Unless you understood the game of chess. Unless you also understood the nature of memory function in a microprocessing unit." He took off his glasses and folded them, and all at once he seemed like some juvenile professor, a prodigy, about to deliver a lecture to an august body. She wanted to laugh but she didn't—how could you laugh when his whole face was so goddamn *intense?*

"If it was checkers, I might be prepared," she said.

"Checkers," he said, barely able to keep the tone of disgust from his voice. He stared at the soldering iron for a moment. "Basically what I'm doing is reprogramming an electronic chess machine by adding to its repertoire of programmed openings. So I'm enlarging the capacity of this hundred-buck unit by adding a whole set of openings." He twisted his head and looked up at her. That gleam in his eye, she thought. Sometimes it seemed wild to her.

"Okay. Enough, enough. I don't understand a word of it, but I'm proud of you anyhow." And she leaned over, kissing the top of his head, then ruffling his hair with the flat of her hand.

"Hey, it's simple, the machine as produced doesn't have the English Opening or the Dutch Defence in its memory, and all I'm doing is adding—"

"English, Dutch." She shrugged. "I just don't want you to pull any more all-nighters, okay?"

"Okay." He sighed, but it was a pretend sigh, a part of the game they played out between one another—a game of affection, of mutual understanding. Something Mike couldn't grasp, couldn't get a handle on, like a secret he was locked out from. *You indulge that kid too much, Kate. You spoil him rotten.* Maybe, she thought. But if love was spoiling, then she was going to spoil. Sometimes, in her innermost darkness, she felt that Peter was all she had. All she would ever have.

"About lunch," she said.

"What lunch?"

"We're having lunch with Mike and his mother—"

"No," Peter said. "Do I have to?"

"You mean you don't *want* to?"

He smiled at her. "She reminds me of an ice cube."

"Are you being fair to ice cubes, Peter?"

"Please," he said. *"Please?"*

She relented. What the hell—he'd only irritate Mike at the lunch table, playing with the saltshaker or the peppermill, spilling something, scribbling on a napkin, or retreating into one of his sullen silences. And she'd see Mike's annoyance grow and grow, like some invisible balloon being puffed up, across the table.

She said, "Okay. But only if you promise me—no more all-nighters, right?"

"Right. Cross my heart."

"I'm not altogether sure you mean it. But I'll make your excuses for you."

He rose and put his arms around her. "Thanks, Mom," he said. "I appreciate it."

3

Somehow she didn't look forward to the sessions with Elliott any more. At one time she'd found some kind of comfort, solace, in sitting in his office and opening up to him, but not now. It had something to do with Mike, his attitudes towards what he called "trick cyclists." He had a wonderful talent for making her feel guilty about analysis. *Look at these bills,* he'd say. *You really think you need this guy? I mean, what's he doing for you? And what the hell is wrong with you anyhow?*

In the back of the cab she folded her hands in her lap, looking down at the skirt of her pale gray suit, the matching gloves. I don't know what's wrong, she thought.

Maybe nothing. Maybe everything. I can't define it for you, Mike, and even if I could you wouldn't want to understand. Satisfaction. Contentment. A sense of passion. These things are missing from my life. Call it by any name you like, it comes down to a certain *emptiness*. A place where everything is dark, like the inside of an impossibly long tunnel. And Elliott tries to find some way to get me out of that place, that's what he does. He listens.

But he isn't really helping she thought.

What you need, Mike had said once, *is a priest. A father confessor. They come cheaper.*

She stared through the window of the cab, twisting her fingers together. She wondered how many other patients began to resent their analysts, began to feel inferior and vulnerable because they'd talked too much, given away too much of themselves with wild generosity, knocked down all their own defences and barriers and received nothing in return except for empty suggestions and occasional prescriptions. You couldn't tell with Elliott what he was thinking as he listened, whether his mind was someplace else, whether he had developed a certain professional glaze so that he could look interested when he was really dreaming of other things.

The cab was pulling into the sidewalk now. She paid, stepped out, conscious suddenly of the immensity of the buildings around her, almost as if they seemed to leap higher and higher in the clear sunlight, thrusting upwards into the heart of the sun. She felt tiny, threatened by the massive architecture, imagining for a moment that the buildings would collapse around her. A mild form of agoraphobia, Elliot had once said. A fear of public places. She went to the private side entrance of the brownstone, glancing at the brass plate with his name on it, then pushed the wooden door open and entered the lobby. She thought: *A neurotic housewife.* It felt like the tag appended to the toe of a corpse in the cold room of the morgue.

She went inside the reception room of Elliott's office. She was perspiring a little, a thin web of sweat forming in her armpits. There was noboby at the reception desk. The receptionist's typewriter had a black dust cover over it.

The waiting room was empty. For a moment she was at a loss. The tiny missing cog in the machine: where was the girl? How would Elliott know she'd arrived if there wasn't anyone to announce her? She looked round the room.

A tidy stack of magazines. The polished surface of a coffee table. A couple of sofas. You could go straight through, she thought. Knock on his door, step right into the inner sanctum. Oh, shit. She gazed at the magazines. Pick one up. Read it. Wait. Something will happen sooner or later. *Harper's. Better Homes and Gardens.* Something she'd never heard of before, *Games.* Why didn't they ever have things like *Screw* or *Hustler* in waiting rooms? Why did they always assume you wanted to flick the pages of *Harper's* and read bitchy reviews or stare at the vacuous living rooms of the ultrarich, rooms in which it was clear nobody really lived, smoked cigarettes, picked their teeth, fornicated on those deep white rugs set in front of vast unlit fireplaces?

She didn't hear Elliott open his door. She didn't hear him come into the reception room.

"Kate."

She turned. She wondered at the strong sense of relief she felt on seeing him. He was smiling at her. Do I depend on him as much as this? she thought. She hated the notion, beset again by a feeling of vulnerability, as though she were a thin sheet of glass he could see through at a glance.

He said, "My receptionist is on vacation. I have to do the honors myself." Still smiling, he turned towards the open door of his office. "I'm not very good at it," he added.

She followed him through. He closed the door after her. This room, she thought, this room with its comfortable chairs and its casual sense of disorder, its overwhelming familiarity—God, she disliked this room so much. She sat down, watching Elliott go around his desk to the damn rocking chair he always sat in. Maybe this is how a junkie feels about his connection, she thought. The whole love-hate deal, the sense of need struggling with the remnants of independence, self-reliance. Self-esteem, Christ. She'd opened herself up to Elliott so many times in this damn room—how could she have any self-esteem left? (He'd say, *That's confused thinking, Kate. The more you tell me, the more esteem you should feel. It takes a little courage to be honest. Or didn't you know that?*)

Courage. She wished she had enough of it to stop coming here.

Elliott watched her in silence for a moment. She was conscious of sunlight, sliced by the open slats of the blind, falling on his meticulous fair hair. He had a handsome face but sometimes she saw something blindingly cold in the blue eyes, something analytical and calculating. The eyes of a judge, maybe. But he'd never made any judgements of her, he'd never passed down any moral law, any code of ethical behavior. Why did she keep expecting him to?

He picked up a silver-plated letter opener, turning it in his hands. He had good hands, she thought. Firm, long fingers, clipped nails. She couldn't imagine him chewing on those nails. But then she couldn't imagine him worrying over anything or slipping into anxiety. Maybe that was it, maybe that's where her feelings lay. She looked at Elliott and what she saw was a kind of perfection, something that highlighted her own inadequacies.

He put the letter opener down and leaned across the desk towards her. "What's been happening since the last time we talked?" he said.

She glanced at him, then down at her hands. Gloves—why was she wearing gloves? Nobody wore gloves these days. Elliott would think: *She's covering something up.* She looked at his face, which was blurred by the stripes of sunlight.

"Nothing much," she said. Feeble. Weak. You can do better than that.

Elliott smiled. "It's funny how you always begin with that phrase. 'Nothing much.' Maybe you think of your visits here the way you'd think of a dentist."

"No—"

"You put me in the position of having to pull teeth, Kate."

She got up from the chair, took off the gloves, walked to the shelves of books. She felt blank. If I say something now, she thought, it's going to be incoherent.

Elliott said, "How are things with Mike?"

She shrugged. "Mike? There's a kind of status quo."

"Like how?"

"I pretend. . . ."

"Pretend what, Kate?"

She stared at the book titles. A number of them were in German, French, Italian. *Jahrbuch für Psychoanalytische Forschungen. Revue Française de Psychanalyse. Archívio generale di Neurologia, Psichiatría e Psicoanalisi.* She had the frightening thought of millions of people all over the world being analysed in foreign languages. The Tower of Babble.

"What do you pretend?" Elliott asked.

"I fake orgasm. I fake tenderness. I fake love." There, it was out in the cold now. "I fake everything, just about."

"Why?"

"I guess it makes him feel good."

"Forget about him, Kate. What makes *you* feel good?"

She went back to her chair and sat down, closing her eyes, listening to the sound of Elliott's steady breathing, the sound of her own heartbeat. The dream, she thought. The dream makes me feel good. She said nothing for a long time. Elliott sighed.

"You don't have an answer for that?" he said.

She opened her purse and took out a cigarette, lighting it with a lighter Thomas had given her years ago, a silver one with her initials engraved on the side. There was a clean ashtray on the table beside her chair. She watched Elliott get up and open the window slightly. Of course, the smoke bothered him. She'd forgotten how much. Why didn't he just hang a NO SMOKING sign on the wall?

"I shouldn't have married him," she said.

"That doesn't exactly answer my question, Kate." He returned to his chair and rocked back and forth slowly, waiting. The chair creaked. The noise irritated her.

"I don't *know* how to answer your question," she said.

"Okay. Okay. Why did you marry him anyway?"

"You get lonely," she said. "You begin to see yourself through the eyes of other people. You look, you see a widow, you see a widow with nothing left to mourn over, you see an empty bed. I mean . . . Mike came along. He filled a gap."

"Was that a good enough reason?"

"Obviously not," she said quickly.

She listened to the silence in the room. Elliott had stopped rocking his chair. She raised her face and looked at him and before she could stop herself she was telling him about the dream. She was telling him about the shower, the man who clamped his hand over her mouth, the gradual yielding of herself to pleasure. . . . His expression didn't change. He listened with his hands clasped on the desk in front of himself.

"Why does he seem familiar to you, Kate?" he asked when she had stopped.

"I don't know. . . . Maybe because I keep having the dream. Not every night. Two, maybe three times a a month. That's all. I guess I should have mentioned it before, except it seemed so goddamn infantile."

"Infantile? I don't think so. I'm interested in why he's familiar, that's all. I mean, does he remind you of anyone you've ever met?"

"No." She could feel it now, the direction this was taking, the suspicion she'd entertained before, but it was wrong, horrible, macabre. It was only a goddamn dream, after all.

"Is there something in the way he touches you?" Elliott asked. "Is there something in the way he *feels*, Kate?"

"I know what you're thinking—"

"I'm not thinking anything."

She got up from her chair. "You are. . . ."

Elliott sat back again. The chair began to rock. It reminded her of an infallible clock smugly ticking seconds away. She imagined it would go on rocking even after Elliott was no longer sitting in it.

"You're thinking it's Thomas, aren't you? That's what crossed your mind, isn't it? You think I'm fucking a dead man in my dream, don't you? Jesus Christ."

"I didn't suggest that. You suggested it. Not me, Kate. If this man in the dream reminds you of Thomas, it's only because the dream is compensatory. It's your way out of the bind of the marriage. It's your way of compensating yourself for Mike's failure in bed. So you create a lover, a rapist, whatever. And he satisfies you. Thomas, somebody else, it doesn't matter. It's nothing to feel shame over—"

"I don't feel any fucking shame!"

"Don't get angry with *me*, Kate. Where does your anger really lie? Mmm? Where does it really lie?"

She shut her eyes. Christ, how she could hate Elliott.

"Maybe it lies with Mike. And with yourself. Maybe you should explain his failings to him."

"Tell him he stinks in bed?"

"If you have to," Elliott said.

She saw him glance at his watch now. The meter was running. The time ticking away. It's like riding in an expensive cab, she thought. And she felt even more annoyed with him.

"There's a wall, Kate. Mike thinks he's satisfactory. You lead him to believe it. Unless you tell him differently, he's going to go on believing it. And when that happens, the whole situation will deteriorate even more."

"Tell the truth and shame the devil," she said.

"Something like that."

"What am I supposed to do? Look into his eyes and say, *know what Mike, you suck in bed?* Could *you* do that in my position?"

"If I had to."

If you had to, she thought. I can't imagine anything in your life, Elliott, that could create adverse situations. I can't imagine you out of control, slave to some emotion, I can't even imagine you taking your goddamn clothes off. So what's the big secret? I'm paying you enough; why don't you tell me? How do I become perfect like you, shrink? Where do I get the blueprint for happiness?

"But you don't have to tell him quite so harshly, do you?" he asked. "You don't have to be so crude. You could find a gentle way of letting him know that the sexual relationship is lacking."

The sexual relationship is lacking. How clinical. How chilly. How utterly pat. *See here, Mike, you don't fuck me well enough, so I have to get my rocks off in a dream, and the screamingly funny thing is that the guy in the dream died years ago. . . .*

She looked down at the pattern of the rug. A line from

some old Bob Dylan song came into her head, something that didn't make much sense: *When gravity fails and negativity won't pull you through.*

Gravity. Negativity.

She looked at Elliott. "Maybe it's me. Maybe there's something wrong with me, not Mike."

"What do you think could be wrong with you, Kate?"

You name it, she thought. "I don't know. I don't attract him, that could be it. I'm not attractive to him."

"Come on," Elliott said. "You're off target."

"You think I'm attractive?"

"Of course I do."

"Would *you* want to sleep with me?"

"Yes. In the right circumstances. You're a very attractive woman."

"The right circumstances," she said. "What would they be?"

Elliott smiled and indicated a photograph on his desk, then reached towards it, turning it around so she could see it. His wife, naturally. Kate saw a woman with a face that was both pretty and severe; there was something tired in the faint smile that lay on her mouth, as if it were less an expression than something she'd chosen to wear for the purpose of a picture. What would it be like to be Elliott's wife? she wondered. Did they sit up in bed at night with their Book-of-the-Month Club selections? Maybe she was more Literary Guild and he Psychology Book Club. She had a sudden picture of Bob and Emily Newhart in their TV bedroom, and she wondered if Elliott's home life was like that sitcom and all at once she wanted to laugh.

"I'm married," he said. "Breach of ethics aside, why would I jeopardize my marriage, and you yours, just because we wanted a few minutes in bed? It doesn't seem worth the risk."

"The question was hypothetical," Kate said. *Breach of ethics!*

"I know it was."

"Sometimes I don't feel attractive. . . ."

"Then you're underestimating your own worth, that's all. You've got to open up to Mike. You've got to get through to him. If you don't, I can't see any future for the marriage."

She nodded. "Open up. Right. I'll try it. I'll try opening up."

"There's no other course, you know that, don't you?"

She turned her gloves around in her hands. "He's a bad listener."

"You've got to make him listen, Kate."

"I'll rope him to a chair."

Elliott smiled. "If you have to. But when you make him understand, I think you'll find the dreams will stop."

I don't want them to stop, she thought. Don't you see that, Elliott? *I don't want the dreams ever to stop.*

"Why don't we make it the same time next week?" Elliott said.

"Sure," she said. In and out, like a bird in a cuckoo clock. And what was she left with at the end of a session? The ordeal of talking to Mike?

He walked with her back into the reception room. He looked at his watch again. He said, "I know I'm cutting this short, but I've got one of those dreadful professional symposiums to attend."

"Take it off my bill," she said.

He looked at her for a time in silence. She noticed a thin line of perspiration on his forehead. (My God, the good doctor sweats. He's a human being and all the time I was under the impression he was a listening device.) He shook her hand curtly and smiled and went back inside his office.

She walked along the corridor thinking of the time she would have to kill before the lunch date—the dreaded lunch date with Mike and Mother Frost.

Shit. She didn't like killing time.

4

Beep. Elliott. This is Bobbi. Remember me? I've got a new shrink now, Elliott. I don't need you. I don't fucking need you. He's going to help me. Not like you. He's called Levy. Maybe you've heard of him? But we're not through yet, Elliott. I'm not finished with you yet. I took something from your office today, Elliott. Guess what? Can't you guess, Doctor big shot shrink? Look in your bathroom. Maybe you'll get warm.

He had switched the tape machine off. *Look in your
bathroom.* He had looked in the bathroom. Just before
Kate Myers had come he had looked inside the medicine
cabinet, staring at the shelves of drug samples, those little
bottles and envelopes left by pharmaceutical salesmen.
Every one a wonder drug. Variations on familiar themes
—chlorpromazine, vasopressin derivatives, carbamaze-
pine. At first he hadn't noticed anything missing. Everything had seemed to be in its place. And then it occurred
to him, the way you sometimes try to name a phrase of
music that drifts through your brain, that something
wasn't in its place. Something. But what?

The razor.

Bobbi had taken his razor.

He'd searched all over for it, panicked, trying to fight
the sensation. But nothing. It was gone. She'd taken it.
Then he'd listened to the tape again, chilled by the sound
of Bobbi's voice: *I'm not finished with you yet.* The
words had stayed in his head all the time Kate Myers had
been in the office. Poor Kate. He'd barely been able to
concentrate on her problems. Even when she'd asked that
strange question, *would you want to sleep with me,* his
sense of arousal, his consciousness of her sexual being,
seemed distant from himself, out of perspective, like the
sensation of another man. Male analyst and female patient, he thought. A slow fuse burning, but you had to
throw cold water on the spark. . . . He'd make it up to
Kate later, maybe with a longer session, but that wasn't
what bothered him now.

It was the thought of that open razor, the blade of
cutting steel, in the hands of somebody like Bobbi. And
that terrible echo, which came again and again through
his mind like an icy tide: *I'm not finished with you yet.*

He had to do something.

Something.

5

The museum was an oasis, a floating island of quiet, as if
it weren't a part of Manhattan but some other dimension
you entered just by stepping through the doorway and pay-

ing the price of admission. Two dollars worth of magic,
Kate thought. Magic and silence, a sense of serenity.
And if you tried hard enough you could forget the noise
of traffic and the blare of the streets. Even in the garden,
which was empty save for two Japanese tourists snapping
Caro's orange steel sculpture on the upper terrace, you
could contrive to forget that you were enclosed in the
city, that it hung in the sky all around you like the bars of
some monstrous prison. She watched the tourists a moment, watched how they went around Caro's "Midday,"
as if intent on photographing it from every possible angle.
Click, click, click. How many more could they take? She
realized she'd never liked that sculpture much anyhow.
Too cold. Too mechanical. It wasn't like midday at all.
She always thought of noon as being warm somehow, even
the word itself suggested hard sunlight, but the sculpture
was cold despite the orange paint.

She paused beside Moore's "Large Torso." She
touched the arched figure with the tips of her fingers, then
looked upwards at the window of her favorite room, the
one she always saved for last. "The Water Lilies." She
moved away from the Moore, staring at the fecundity of
Lachaise's "Standing Woman." Sexual. Huge hips. Large
breasts. The earth mother, she thought. You wanted to
put your arms around the woman because you knew you
would feel safe. Silly, she thought. A sculpture. She went
close to it but didn't touch it. She imagined it would be
cold to touch and what she wanted to retain was its
impression of warmth. Overhead, churning the air, a
helicopter crossed the sky. The whir of the blades slashing
irritated her, that and the clicking of the tourists' camera.
God, I'm edgy, she thought. Why am I always edgy when
I come from Elliott's office? Then there was the prospect
of lunch. *How are you today, Katherine?* Never Kate.
*Mike tells me you're still seeing an analyst. My goodness.
What is he trying to cure you of?* Hell. I could ram a
breadstick down her throat. There, mother-in-law, choke
on that baby.

She went back inside the building, moving towards the
stairs. It was then she realized somebody was following
her, somebody was moving behind her; the same person

must have been in the garden just beyond her view. No,
she thought. That's so stupid. Nobody is following me.
She glanced behind her. A man. A man apparently study-
ing a catalogue in his hand as he climbed the stairs. He
isn't interested in me, she thought. He isn't following me.
She saw his eyes move from the catalogue to her face,
then she turned away. Hadn't Elliott just told you you're
an attractive woman? Why wouldn't the guy be interested . . . ?

Interested in what?

Picking you up?

Then maybe he's only *pretending* to be interested in
that catalogue.

She paused in front of Rousseau's "The Dream." A
jungle. She thought she could lose herself in that green-
ery, that lushness, because it didn't seem remotely menacing to her, more welcoming, as if it were saying: *It's
okay, you can step inside, nothing in this dream will harm
you, Kate.*

What would you do if he tried to pick you up? Something tremendously Victorian, like slapping his face with
a glove? Or would you go along just for the sheer hell of
it? She turned slowly and looked around the room. He
was still there, several yards away, looking at the catalogue absently, in such a way that suggested he wasn't
really reading it, that he was actually watching her from
the corner of his eye. She moved on, pausing in front of
Ensor's "Masks Confronting Death." This one always
frightened her—those blurred faces staring out at you,
like they were about to enter hell, like they were inviting
you to come along and yet warning you at the same time.
She stared at it for a time, then she heard a movement
behind her. She turned, looked quickly, saw the guy
glance at her. The lock of eyes lasted a moment then he
looked away, he looked away as if he hadn't noticed her
at all.

It's a game, she thought suddenly. It's the game of the
pickup. She felt suddenly warm, attractive, drawn towards the secret nature of the game. For a moment she
had the urge to cross the floor and speak with him
directly and say something like: *Admit it, admit how*

attractive you find me, go on. . . . But now he was flicking the pages of his catalogue again. She stared at him, waiting for him to look at her again, realizing all at once that the catalogue he held in his hands was upside down, that it was nothing more than a meaningless item of apparatus in the game. Upside down, for Christ's sake! She looked at his face, a square face with a jaw that seemed strong and firm, a skull covered with dark curly hair, and for a moment she imagined holding that face against her breasts, feeling his breath upon her skin. *What the hell am I doing? Hoping he picks me up?* The tragic cliche. FLASH: NEUROTIC HOUSEWIFE FUCKS STRANGER, MUSEUM PICKUP INDICATED. She caught her breath, which was tight in her throat, and tried to relax. *A perfect stranger—is that what you really want, Kate? The dream lover who comes alive in the museum in the afternoon, as if he'd managed to pass from one dimension to the next, from the other world of sleep into reality?*

"Three Women," by Leger.

She stared at it, trying to figure it out, trying to make connections of a rational kind between the disjointed shapes. She looked at her watch. 11:30. There was still plenty of time to spend in the museum. Plenty of time before the lunch.

"They don't look like any women I ever met."

He was standing right beside her now. She didn't look at him. She smiled quickly, nodded in agreement, glanced down at the catalogue he held in his hands—upside down still. His fingers were long, square at the tips, hair grew along the back of his hands.

"I mean, I wouldn't want to date one of them," he said. He had a deep voice, the kind you could imagine reading the news on a radio. "Go into a restaurant with one of them, people would stare."

She nodded her head again, trying despairingly to think of something to say. Caught between wanting to talk with him and wanting to avoid him, she felt a pulse flutter at the back of her throat. *Show him the wedding ring,* she told herself. *Make it conspicuous. Make it obvious that you're off limits to all but privileged personnel. Namely, Mike. Namely, your dream rapist . . .* She couldn't think of a goddamn thing to do except go on shaking her head, as if no matter what he said she would agree.

She moved away, half-smiling, passing into the room that contained Chagall's "Calvary," a painting she liked because it suggested a suffering beyond words, a supreme suffering. She stared at it for a time, then realized she wasn't really seeing it; she was waiting for the man to reappear, waiting for him to tear himself away from the three disjointed figures, waiting for him to make a direct approach, wondering what it would be like. . . . *Pssst, want to fuck? Got twenty minutes to kill?* Or something crazy in its irony: *I have these etchings, of all things . . .* Etchings, itchings. But he didn't appear in the gallery and she felt suddenly low, disappointed, as if some tacit agreement had been broken, violated. Then she thought: You're out of your tree, Kate, entertaining some wicked fantasy, killing time with sexual fluff. But then why the hell did she feel disappointed?

She moved on, entering the room she saved for the last. Monet's "Water Lilies." The enormous canvasses that suggested an idyll. A room of silence, peace, tranquility. She sat down, lost herself in the colors of the paintings for a time, then turned to the window overlooking the garden. The Japanese tourists were still taking pictures, having moved from the Caro to Maillol's "The River," with its upended female figure. They were pointing, snapping, gesticulating wildly. She watched them for a time, then she closed her eyes.

It was the peacefulness that brought her here time and again—the silence, which was a tangible thing enclosed by these enormous painting. She could float through it, wallow in it, pretend she wasn't in the city, in any city, that she existed for a moment outside the limitations of space and time, outside the boundaries of herself.

She opened her eyes. She stared across the room at the empty doorway. He isn't coming, she thought. Why isn't he coming? Why do you want him to come anyhow? Just an empty doorway, an empty gallery. She looked down at her hands, seeing how they were made into tight fists. I want him to try again, she thought. *That's what I want. . . .*

A stranger, for God's sake.

You didn't pick up a stranger, not if you were in your right mind.

Then she noticed something that shocked her, the sight of a vast stain covering the rug around her seat: discoloration, as if rain had leaked through the roof during a storm. How could such a thing have happened in this wonderful room? She raised her eyes to the ceiling. There were brown watermarks, the color of old rust, on the tiles. How could it have happened in this room, *her* room? And then she noticed that the vast window was cracked, that the spidery crack had been covered over with transparent tape. Not in *this* room. A defilement, her own private space vandalized by nature. Cracked glass. Stains. She got up from the seat quickly just as the man stepped into the gallery.

He was looking at her across the room.

She turned her face to the side, gazing at the Monets.

You want him, you don't want him. . . .

Blow on the fine filaments of a dandelion. Watch them drift away like unfulfilled wishes.

"This is my favorite room also. . . ."

She stared at him. Why had he said that? How could he have known that this was her favorite room too? He moved slowly towards her. She wondered: What would it be like to fuck here in this room of water lilies, to give yourself up to this stranger, to stretch back on the sofa and let him enter you and feel the soft impression of the paintings fade beneath your closed eyelids?

The stain. The cracked window. They spoiled the place for her.

She moved towards the door, passing him, trying to avoid his outstretched hand, the feeling of his fingertips brush against her wrist. Leave me alone, she thought. Leave me in peace. *I don't want you.* . . .

She heard him calling to her. But she didn't stop. She went quickly through the various galleries, reaching the stairs, still hearing him call after her. *Hey, lady, lady . . .* She went down the stairs. At the bottom she paused. She looked across the foyer. She saw traffic passing in the street outside. She saw an art student check his briefcase into the cloakroom, a security guard, arms folded, standing alongside the admissions desk. Go up to the guard, she thought. Tell him there's a guy bothering you. Tell him. Just go straight up to him. . . .

Why don't you?

She shut her eyes a second and she thought: Because you don't want to, that's why.

She stepped back into the garden again, flustered, stopping beside the "Standing Woman"—all that ripeness, that readiness, that wild suggestion of willingness. You want him to pick you up. You want him. She looked down at her hands. One glove, only one glove held in the palm. She must have dropped the other someplace, maybe on the stairs, in one of the galleries. What the hell, it didn't matter now. She looked up at the sky, conscious of the enormity of it. It made her feel momentarily dizzy. Then she went back inside the building. You're not looking for the lost glove, she thought. You're looking for *him*.

No, Kate.

It's stupid, absurd, you don't even know him.

She gazed across the foyer.

He wasn't there. Only the security guard, the girl at the admissions desk, a woman staring out absently from the cloakroom. But no sign of him. . . .

Why didn't she feel relief?

Why was there only a sense of letdown, of sinking?

And then she saw him, she saw him moving towards the front door, saw the glass flash in sunlight as the door swung open then shut. She moved after him. Outside, the sun was hot on her face, more like some enraged tropical sun than any you might find in the city. It seemed swollen and bruised, distended, as if some refraction of light, some weird atmospheric condition, had distorted it. Stop, she thought. Don't go any further. There's a lunch, people are expecting you, there are rules of behavior you're supposed to obey, there are limitations on what you can do and what you can't— He was hailing a cab on the other side of the street. She saw one pull next to the sidewalk. She watched him open the door and get inside— and then, through the open window of the back compartment, he was staring at her and smiling. He lifted one hand in the air, holding something. The glove. The glove. Was that all? Was that it? He just wants to return the goddamn glove? She felt empty again. She watched him. The cab hadn't moved. He was waiting for her.

You don't have to cross this street. You don't need the goddamn glove. All you have to do now is turn and walk the other way and pretend nothing ever happened, pretend you never met the guy, never hoped he'd pick you up, pretend it was nothing more than some escapist fantasy you used to pass away the time. The lunch. Oh, Christ, the lunch. *Mike looks like he's lost some weight, Katherine. Aren't you feeding him properly?* Mike nodding, smiling, solicitous. The old bat's face, the breadsticks peppered with sesame seeds, the ritual of calling a waiter. And she always complained about something. She looked for complaints.

To hell with the lunch, she thought.

To hell with all of it.

She crossed the street to the waiting cab. The door was opened for her. She wanted to say something, but the only thing that came into her mind was ridiculous. *I think you have my glove. See? It matches this one, so it must be mine, so maybe I can have it back.* But the man, saying nothing, reached for her wrist and drew her down against him, laughing quietly to himself. Something in her wanted to resist, wanted to struggle against him, but she realized she had no control over events, no power to resist. He didn't kiss her, he just held her against him so that her face was pressed to the side of his, and she was aware of the smell of fading after-shave, a musk. The cab was moving away from the sidewalk. And then his mouth was against hers, a strange sensation, the deep kiss of somebody you didn't know, somebody you wanted nevertheless, the touch of teeth, tongue against tongue, and—as in the dream—she yielded, she gave herself, looking for that dark delicious place, silent as the floor of some mythic ocean, where nothing made any sense but the surge of your own desire.

He drew his face away. She felt his hand under her skirt, pressed to the inside of her thigh.

"What kept you?" he said.

She didn't answer. She opened her mouth, raised her hand to the side of his face, and kissed him again, losing herself in the depth of the kiss.

I spy with my little eye. . . .

The tall blonde woman with the outsized dark glasses and the shoulder purse watched the cab slide away from the curb. At the end of the street it stopped at a red light. Dear Doctor Elliott, she thought. Dear, sweet, mother-fucking shrink, you'll pay. God, how you'll pay. In flesh and blood, bastard: in all the flesh and blood it takes.

TWO

1

It was the relentless sound of the telephone that, like some demented bird, woke Liz from a dreamless sleep. When she opened her eyes, seeing a slit of cruel sunlight through the drapes, she remembered coming home at dawn, dropping a Placidyl, crawling exhausted into bed, then the relief of sleep, the comfort of that solid dark wall. She closed her eyes against the sunlight and reached out for the telephone on the bedside table, her hand colliding with a half-empty glass of water. Shit. The water slopped across the table, around a box of Kleenex, then dripped on to the rug. She sat upright and wondered why she still felt so god-awful tired, like the weariness was in the marrow of her bones—not something you could exorcise with simple chemical wizardry. Her legs ached, the calves especially. The base of her spine felt sore too. Coming apart at the seams, she thought. Like a bargain basement bra. What could you expect after last night? She held the telephone in one hand while with the other she lightly massaged the muscle of her right calf.

"This is a recorded message from the morgue," she said. "Liz is presently in a condition approximating death. When you hear the beep—"

"Crap."

"Norma?"

"Norma," the voice said.

"Why don't you call me back, huh?" The shitting sunlight. It struck the lids of her eyes with the intensity of lit matches.

"No can do, baby," the voice said.

"I'm beat. B–e–a–t. Beat."

"Spelling I'm good at, Liz. You got a pencil handy?"

Liz opened her eyes and looked at the puddle of water

35

on the slick surface of the table. Sodden Kleenexes, a wet Bic pen, some crumpled scraps of paper, cigarette butts. Make something out of that little collection, she thought. The pen wouldn't write and the paper was sticking to the water. A cop could come in, someone with a sharp eye for these details, and survey her body and say: *Tell you one thing, she wasn't big on keeping her bedroom tidy*.

"You ready?" Norma said.

"No, but shoot anyhow."

Norma read out an address in the West Seventies, an apartment number, a name. "You want me to repeat that?"

Liz looked at the indentations she'd made with the useless Bic on the soaking paper. "I think I got it."

"Read it back to me, love."

Liz did so, squinting at the piercing sunlight. Why was everything so goddamn bright? You'd think whoever arranged these things—the weather, the hours, the changing of seasons—would have some consideraton for the condition of *homo sapiens*. You feel awful so you get a blinding shot of sunshine. You feel really good and you get a million gallons of rain.

"What time?" she asked. She stuck the Bic between her lips.

"Four thirty."

"And what time is it now?"

"Three minutes past noon."

"Three minutes past noon?" Liz said. "Is that all?"

"Now four minutes, according to my digital."

"Thanks for the precision," Liz said.

"Texas Instruments, you know."

Liz put the telephone down then lay back with her eyes shut. There was a suggestion of a headache now, a faint pounding somewhere deep inside her skull. The small guy with the hammer. Sometimes he had a buzz saw. There had been champagne last night. The guy from Dallas seemed to like the stuff—a Dom Perignon, one bottle after another. Then it occurred to her that maybe Norma had been making one of her little jokes, a tiny pun. Texas Instruments. Well, hell, she was always catching Norma's jokes a second too late. She turned on her side. The guy from Dallas, before fading into a drunken stupor, had mentioned something about a certain stock. Why was she having this difficulty in remembering the name? *It's going to go up, baby, faster'n a rocket on the Fourth of July.* What was its goddamn name?

Auto something.

Auto what?

She rose and wandered into the bathroom and, sticking her head inside the shower stall, turned on the cold-water spray. The shock was terrible. She moaned, pulled her face away from the stream, wrapped her hair in a towel. She walked into the kitchen, opened the refrigerator, took out a can of orange juice and popped the top. The stuff tasted vile, acidic, like it was vinegar. She sat down at the table, lit a cigarette, gazed at the white sun on the window. *Baby needs her vitamins.* Through the fog she could hear the echo of her mother's voice. *Baby needs this, baby needs that.* (Auto what? Auto-Tech? Auto-Flagellation?) Why, when she felt low, did she always hear an echo of her mother? Guilt, what else? The other side of that abominable currency they called The Puritan Work Ethic. She sipped some more of the orange juice, made a face, pushed the little can away. It was the letters that did it, of course. Once a week, with a regularity that was dreadful, they came from Chicago. The crabbed handwriting on the envelope, the cheerful platitudes inside, the maternal warnings about the perils of the big city (as if Chicago were a hick town). *I know you like your work, dear, and I know how good it makes you feel to teach remedial reading to those black kids, but I worry about whether you're looking after yourself.*

Remedial reading! *The Remedial Reading Escort Service, Discretion Guaranteed.* She put out her cigarette in the garbage disposal unit, flipped the switch, listened to the blades grate. Sometimes she imagined going back to Chicago, sitting down in that cluttered shaded room her mother insisted on calling a "Parlor," and just coming out with the truth about Baby. See, Mom, it's like this. I'm not really involved in education, at least not as you understand that word. My work is more along the lines of, well, ahem, hum, *social* intercourse? She tried to picture her mother's face. The blank look. Incomprehension. *My baby is a——?*

Frankly, yes. A simple matter of economics, Mom.

Dream on, Liz.

She looked inside the refrigerator again. Apart from another can of orange juice, two eggs—one of which was cracked—an empty jar that had once contained wheat germ, and an old piece of a submarine sandwich, there was nothing. Her mother would die if she looked inside this machine. A nutritionist's nightmare. She shut the door again. She looked at the kitchen clock. 12:19. Then she wondered if she could go back to sleep again, but it seemed pointless. She thought about the guy from Dallas. He'd worn a suit he might have ripped off from a museum dedicated to the relics of the life of Hank Williams. Fluted pockets in the shapes of arrows. New Texan money. You could smell it on his flesh. The folds of his clothing. It hung around him like some angelic aura.

She walked into the living room, sat down on the sofa, stared around. She never felt at home in this room. It had a sense of a glossy photograph to it, something you looked at but didn't actually participate in. Unlike the bedroom, it was neat and ordered. Even the ashtrays were empty, shining. Closing her eyes, crossing her legs, feeling the same muscular twinge as before, she sat back. Auto-Tron! That was it. *I swear by it, I really do.*

She reached forward to the coffee table and picked up the telephone, punching numbers. The snooty girl in Max's office answered; she always did so with the kind of arrogance that suggested she was speaking through a gauze germproof wrap round the mouthpiece.

"Liz Blake. Let me talk to Max."

"I'll see if he's available, Miss Blake. Please hold."

Scratching. Buzzing. Then Max was on the other end of the line. He had one of those sonorous voices you associate with radio reports of distant wars.

"How's the street, Max?" she said.

"Inscrutable as ever," he answered.

"A question. What is AutoTron going for?"

"AutoTron. Hang on. Let me look." There was a shuffling of papers. She pictured Max in his untidy office; despite his voice, he had the appearance of a gnome, a leprechaun, dwarfed by the stacked papers on his desk.

"AutoTron, AutoTron, AutoTron. Let me see." He

paused, and there was more shuffling and crackling. "You got a tip or something?"

"The horse's mouth, my dear."

"Ah. Here we are. AutoTron stands in the current trading at fifteen-sixty. One five six oh."

"What do you know about it?"

"Expanding company. Light industry. Electronic components mainly. Based chiefly in Fort Worth. It's been pretty steady lately. No great dramas. If it's a roller coaster ride you want, kid, this isn't the one."

"Since when did I speculate, sweetheart?" Liz said. "Whatever else I may have, I don't have the soul of a gambler." She paused. Where was her calculator? She couldn't find it. "How many can I buy for a grand, Max?"

"A grand." She could hear him shuffle paper again, presumably looking for his calculating machine. Then he was tapping buttons. "Sixty-four, leaving you with small change."

"Go ahead then. Do it for me."

"You want me to sell something to meet it?"

"No, listen, I'll get the cash to you tomorrow, okay?"

"You got it."

"Thanks, Max." And she hung up. She wandered around the room for a time, wondering what the word of a drunken Texan was worth on the open market. It better be good, baby, she thought. She stood at the window and looked down into the street. Two years, she thought. She had given herself two years to get in and out of this game. Invest and save, save and invest, and don't squander a single opportunity. After that she would get out fast. But suddenly two years seemed like a hell of a long time, a huge slice out of the surface of your life. Then she was thinking of her mother again—a picture she didn't want to entertain. It's only for two years, she said to herself. Then you can come in out of the cold . . . come in to what? back to what?

A business of some kind. Something the two years would bankroll. She hadn't figured it out yet.

Turning from the window, she sighed. Zest for life, she thought, where are you when I need you most? She went back inside the bedroom and began to rummage through

the closet for something to wear. She looked at herself in
the full-length mirror and what she saw was someone still
pretty, someone with the kind of good looks that suggest
a certain innocence—the kind of appearance you might
associate with a former candidate for the title of The
Illinois Soybean Producers' Pageant Queen. All I need,
she thought, is a sash, a dress of virginal white, and that
spacey glassy smile that could only be the direct result
of a lobotomy.

She made a face at her own reflection, then moved
away from the mirror.

2

There was a public telephone on the corner opposite the
apartment building. As she dialled the number she looked
through the dirty glass at the concrete structure: a dark
city bird, a pigeon, flew in an awkward way from a
window ledge, flapping, appearing too heavy for flight. She
dropped two coins in the slot, still watching the bird as it
vanished somewhere overhead. From the center of the
street there was an abrupt gust of steam, which billowed
away in a broken ribbon in the late afternoon sunlight.
She put the receiver back down and heard her coins
clatter back down the chute. She took off her dark glasses
for a moment and rubbed her eyes. Earlier, there had
been fear, the far edge of anger, but she had gone beyond
that now; now she didn't feel anything unless she started
to think about Elliott, but why the fuck should she give
Elliott head room? She flipped the pages of a tattered
directory; yellow at one time, the pages were bleached to
a grubby white. Hotels, hotels. She found the number of
The Americana, put more money in the slot, dialled.
She asked to speak to room six oh nine. She waited. Then
she heard the man's voice.

"Walter?" she said.

"Who is this?"

"You don't remember?"

A pause. Then he said, "Bobbi?"

"Right." She slipped her dark glasses on. She watched
a news vendor rush past with a bunch of papers under his
arm. "I'm sorry about last night."

He was quiet again. "It's okay. I guess I came on too strong, didn't I?"

"It was my fault," she said.

"It wasn't anyone's fault."

"No, it was mine. I couldn't . . ." She forgot what she was going to say: her mind was suddenly empty.

She heard him laugh. "Look, honey, I'm a hick. I don't know the score exactly. I misjudged the situation, that's all. What do I know? Huh? Pocatello Walter, what do I know?"

She waited. A moving truck rumbled along the street; she saw the sign MAYFLOWER. She wanted to say, You don't understand, Walter. You don't understand why I ran the way I did. You don't even *begin* to understand. I can't make you see.

"You're checking out today?" she said. She gazed across at the apartment building once more. Somebody passed in front of an upper window.

"Yeah. In about twenty minutes. Matter of fact, you were lucky to catch me."

"All I wanted was to say sorry," she said.

"Listen. You got a number? Maybe I can call you if I get the chance to come back again? We'll take it slower next time—"

She hung up. She laid her face against the cold glass of the box. Next time, she thought. How could she tell about next times? About any times? Sometimes the future was as inscrutable as a deck of cards laid face down. Sometimes she didn't think there was a future—or if there was, then she didn't have any control over it. She wasn't like Elliott. Elliott had control. Control over everything.

She felt angry again. It wasn't a hot thing now, more a feeling of ice, more like she was looking at the sensation from a point outside of herself. *I don't want to think about you, Elliott. Fuck you.*

Somebody rapped on the glass with a coin. "Lady, you using that phone?"

Bobbi stared at the face outside. A small red face with the kind of abrasive quality you saw sometimes on New Yorkers. Why didn't they just wear labels? she wondered: *It's me against the world.* hang a fucking slogan round their necks.

"What does it look like I'm doing?" she said.

"Lady, it's hard to tell."

She knocked the door shut with her knee and picked up the receiver again. Then she shoved more coins in and pressed the familiar digits. Dear Christ. Why was he never in his goddamn office? *Beep.* His flat foreign voice followed by that beep. She hated that sound. And what she remembered all at once was crying into the telephone while the tape turned, sobbing and pouring it all out while the machine recorded it, understanding how ridiculous she was being—nobody is listening, there's nothing there but a telephone answering device, not a person, just a gadget and a strip of magnetic tape, for Christ's sake. *Why, Elliott?* Again and again she'd asked that question. *Why, Elliott? Why won't you allow it? What have I ever done to you?* But that was a long time ago and she wasn't going to be that vulnerable again, not in front of him. Besides, she had Levy now, and Levy was different, kinder, more like some half-forgotten uncle.

She pinched her nostrils, making her voice thin and nasal, thinking it might pass as an impersonation of him. She said, "I can't allow it, Bobbi. I don't see any real grounds for it. I have to have strong grounds, Bobbi, and you're not actually giving me any, are you?" She laughed into the receiver. "Was that close, Elliott? Did that sound like you?" Then she paused, looking across at the apartment building. The windows were all empty, flat empty rows of glass. They reflected the orange of the late sunlight. "I guess you found what I took, didn't you? You looked in the bathroom and you found it, right? I should say, you *didn't* find it. That would be more correct, *actually*. More grammatical, *actually*. Wouldn't it, Elliott? Then you ask yourself, I wonder what she's going to do with my razor? Right again? She's off-the-wall and she has a razor and she's out there somewhere. . . . You don't like that thought, do you? But you don't know where to find me." She paused again, then she sang the same phrase in a tuneless way. *"You don't know where to find me."*

She slammed the receiver down. She adjusted the strap of her purse. Then she stepped out of the telephone booth. The man on the sidewalk, muttering something about dames to himself, brushed past her and shut the glass door. She stood on the edge of the sidewalk, staring at the entrance to the apartment building, smiling to herself in the manner of someone with a secret too deep, too arcane, to share.

She walked slowly across the street.

3

Liz rode in the elevator to the fifth floor; in the burnished wood she could see a dim image of herself. Raising her face, she saw that there was a mirror set in the ceiling of the elevator. The reflection seemed to diminish her and she wondered why, even after all this time, she still felt faintly nervous about going to somebody's apartment. Odd—she shouldn't have been bothered by it now. Maybe it was the same with an actress, stepping on to a stage to speak the same lines night after night; maybe you never quite got over the swarm of butterflies, no matter how many times you went through the same experience. Then she wondered if she looked okay, glancing once more at herself in the overhead mirror—hell, half the time nobody noticed. Half the time they were too drunk to care or too egotistical to notice, wanting to talk about themselves. (*Pittsburgh, right, lived there all my life. Nice place. You want to see a picture of the old homestead?*)

The elevator stopped. She got out. She walked along the corridor. The apartment number—shit, what the hell was it? She searched in her purse for the piece of paper on which she'd scraped the number with the useless ballpoint. Pausing under a lamp, she tilted the paper so she could read it. *Five two four.* What are you like, five two four? She stopped in front of the door, took a compact mirror from her purse, stared at herself quickly (too much lipstick?), and then pressed the buzzer. Almost at once, as if the guy were waiting on the other side, the door was jerked open. He was a man of medium height, nondescript features, but he looked okay—as far as you could tell from surfaces. Sometimes you got the creeps, the weirdos, or highrollers with fat billfolds and an interest in Nazi souvenirs, leathers, wetsuits, riding crops. All that stuff made her sick. Sometimes she'd thought, with surprise: Hey, I'm straight, no kinks, look at me.

She stepped inside the apartment. The guy closed the door.

"I'm Liz," she said. *Fly me to the moon.*

"Ted," the man said.

"Good to know you." She looked round the apartment quickly. Average place, lived-in, nothing fancy. The guy wasn't rich, he wasn't poor; just another In-Between. For a moment she looked at the far wall where some kind of religious icon hung. She went closer to it: a small plaster cast of the Virgin Mary, gaudy in color, the lips bright red and the eyes too blue to be real—like the kind of souvenir you imagined pouring out of Mexican factories in their millions.

The man laughed in an embarrassed way. "It's not mine," he said.

"No?"

"It's not even my apartment. I borrowed it from a friend. He's in Maine and I'm only in town for a day or two. . . ."

It's okay. Save the lengthy explanations, she thought. Then she sensed it in the air, his nervousness, a certain tension, the need to ramble on to no real purpose. She turned away from the little statue and smiled at him. The designer of the figure had contrived to make Christ's mother look like a Tijuana hooker. Some kind of achievement in that, she thought.

"You never used the service before?" she asked.

"No, not exactly," he said. He had his hands in the pockets of his pants.

"They told you what I did and what I didn't do?" she said.

He nodded. "It's okay," he said, almost in a whisper. "I don't have any . . . well, what you might call exotic needs."

"Where's the bedroom?" she asked.

"Um, that door there."

She went briskly towards it. She pushed it open, stepped inside, moved towards the window. The drapes

were drawn; red cotton burning in the slipping-down sun.
Neat: the bedspread matched the drapes and the drapes
matched the rug. A blood-red room. She thought she
remembered it from a nightmare. She called out, "Hey,
are you coming through?"

He shuffled into the doorway. She sat down on the
bed, watching him; he was as wary as some animal whose
life has been one of avoiding larger predatory beasts. The
meek were supposed to inherit something, she thought.
She couldn't remember what it was exactly. She smiled at
him: the full dazzle this time, the come-on.

"Sit down. Here. Beside me." She patted the bedspread.

He moved cautiously towards her.

"Did they tell you I got over my leprosy?" she said.

He stared at her for a moment. She could hear the
penny drop in his head. Then he smiled.

"Cured. Completely cured."

"Yeah," he said. He watched her as she undid the
buttons of her blouse. "Let me do that," he said. "Is it
okay if I do that?"

"Feel free," she answered.

She watched his fingers tremble with her buttons. He
was hopeless. She had to help him, first with the buttons,
then with the buckle of her belt. With any luck, she
thought, this could be a severe outbreak of premature
ejaculation and I could be gone before the statutory hour
had faded away. . . . She lay back across the bedspread
in her underwear, watching him hover above her. There
were times when this was the worst moment, when all the
fears you'd managed to keep hidden came like bats to the
surface. Maybe he'd pull pantyhose from his pocket and
wrap them around your neck, or pull a switchblade and
stick it between your ribs. There were those times when,
at your most vulnerable, you wanted to shut your eyes
and drift away and imagine there was nobody else in the
room with you, you were all alone; sometimes you imagined an old lover, somebody familiar and boring and
wonderfully *safe*. Melvin Pike, for example. Sweet old
Melvin, who had taken that graceful flower called virgini-
ty one bitingly cold Chicago night beneath the bleachers

at the high-school football field. Fumbling Melvin, who could no more catch a pass than he could cut it as a lover. What she suddenly remembered now was the overpowering smell of his sulphurous acne cream and how she wanted to be sick and how quickly he'd shuddered and come and gasped like some beached fish. Dear old Melvin. He'd become a corporation lawyer and married Anita Semler and they had a house in Des Moines, two kids, an English sheepdog, and a parakeet.

She raised her head and looked at the guy. With his back to her, his spine inclined slightly, he was undressing, slipping his pants off. His legs were thin and white, but in the sunlight that came through the red cotton drapes they seemed blotchy, as if he suffered from some skin ailment.

Hurry, she thought. He turned to the bed, still bent a little at the hips in the fashion of someone undergoing an attack of shame. He was erect and his hands, dangling, masked the erection. She wanted to say, *Look, I've seen it all before.* But she said nothing, waiting for him to reach her in silence. He sat on the edge of the bed and slipped the strap of her bra from her shoulder and, moaning a little, leaned to kiss the side of her neck. A moaner, she thought. She felt his hands tug at the bra and she wondered how much of her two years she had left. Fourteen months? Thirteen?

She put her arms up around his shoulders and pulled him down.

The next bit was the trick, the whole magic show. How to distance yourself from the customer while maintaining the delicate illusion of participation. How to be yourself and not yourself, simultaneously. A juggling act. She shifted her hips underneath him, glanced at his face, saw the earnest expression locked into the features. She felt almost sorry for him for a moment, like she was a nurse with a terminal patient.

Think stocks, think shares, she told herself. Think of your bank balance and Wall Street and Max in his little office. Then you won't have time for the creeping affliction of sympathy.

She listened to the guy grunt.

Sometimes it was hard to be the complete materialist.

4

The time, the goddamn time, how had the time slipped so quickly away? She reached for her watch and it slithered from her fingers to the floor, taking with it the wedding ring she'd removed and laid on the bedside table, so she had to go down on her hands and knees to pick them up again and the ring, that small gold hoop Mike had given her with such awful solemnity, had disappeared under the bed. She felt for it, her fingers touching a pair of rolled-up socks, a sandal, an item of discarded clothing. In the darkened room she squinted at the watch—it was five twenty. The afternoon had evaporated. And the lunch, Christ, she'd missed the lunch. Mike would be furious. An excuse, she thought. You need an excuse. *I picked up this guy, Mike, I don't even know his name, I was in the Museum and something kinda came over me and the next thing we were in a cab and we spent the afternoon in bed and I had a terrific time, Mike, the sort of time I don't get from you. . . .* She couldn't think of one. She felt only a weird panic, like a paralysis of the brain. *We fucked, Mike, and it all began in the taxi, and then there was the missing glove. . .* She walked up and down the bedroom, looking at the figure of the sleeping man, the dark hair spread on the rumpled white pillow, the tiny curled hairs that crisscrossed his chest and looked like small tattoos in the half-light. She wanted to wake him, say something to him, but she didn't. All she could think of was going home, facing Mike, an excuse, an excuse. But why couldn't she get her head to respond? She went inside the bathroom and ran cold water and splashed it across her face and she wondered: Will Mike know? Will he know just by looking at me? Is there some kind of sign? A light in the eye, something out of place?

She switched on the light. She picked up a hairbrush from the counter around the sink and ran it quickly through her hair, but it didn't look right. I don't have time, she thought. I don't have time to make myself neat or meticulous. She shivered and returned to the bedroom, picking up her clothes from the floor. She dressed hurriedly, fighting with the panic, thinking: What did I do?

Why am I here? And then on some other level there was
a sense of shame, not of regret, just shame, and then she
couldn't think what to say to Mike, as if the confusion
and the shame were one and the same.

No underwear.

No underwear. She moved around the bed, searched
the floor, wanted to turn on the lamp but didn't because
for some reason she didn't want to wake the man. No
underwear. . . . And then it came to back to her. The
cab.

No.

That couldn't be. She couldn't have left them in the
cab.

She closed her eyes, tried to remember, recalling how
his hand had gone under her pale gray skirt, how the skirt
had been pushed up to her thighs, how torn she'd been
between her own urgent excitement and the cabbie's eyes
in the rearview mirror.

The cab. She must have left them in the cab.

She twisted her hands together, feeling disgust. The
cabdriver. The eyes in the mirror. He must have been
watching. How could he have pretended otherwise? And
the man, teasing her with his fingers, laughing sometimes
as if he'd understood her hunger and how easily he could
control it, satisfy it.

She moved up and down the room. She couldn't find
the underwear. She couldn't even remember the color of
the panties. She strapped the wristwatch around her wrist,
then she looked back at the man—the way he turned in
his sleep, as if he were about to wake and push the
bedsheets aside and tell her to get back in beside him. I
would do it too, she thought. I wouldn't hesitate. No, she
told herself. You can't stay here. You have to leave. You
wish you could wake him and tell him how good it was,
but you don't have time for that.

She walked out of the bedroom. She moved across the
thick rug of the darkened living room. She found a lamp,
turned it on, saw the light gleam in the chromium of the
modernistic furniture. Something, she thought. There's
something I've forgotten. She couldn't think what. That
emptiness again, the mind just draining away. She gazed
at the coffee table, the desk set against the wall by the

door. She thought: I don't even know his name. She went towards the desk. There were a couple of envelopes, windowed envelopes containing bills. Warren Lockman, the name read, but somehow she couldn't associate the name with the man asleep in the bedroom. They were separate entities. Then she wished she hadn't bothered to discover his name, she wished it had remained unknown, a wonderful secret. . . .

She saw another piece of paper lying alongside the envelope, half-buried, an official-looking form of some kind. She pulled it out from the pile and looked at the heading: NEW YORK CITY HEALTH DEPARTMENT. For a moment it didn't dawn on her, the dark print blurred in front of her eyes, she wanted to crush the paper, crumple it, set it alight. WARREN LOCKMAN. I don't know anyone by that name, she thought. I never met anybody called Warren Lockman. Just a man, an afternoon lover. INFECTIOUS VENEREAL DISEASES. No, she thought. LIST OF ALL—

The paper was bent. She couldn't read the rest of it without unfolding the form. She didn't want to do that. LIST OF ALL—

How could she belong to the list of somebody she'd never even met, for God's sake? She turned the paper over. LIST OF ALL—

But the dark print was liquid again, black water, ink spilled over paper and turning into Rorschach blots in the margins. SEXUAL CONTACTS TWO WEEKS PRIOR TO INFECTION. THEY MUST BE NOTIFIED AND EXAMINED FOR GONNORHEA. She let the paper slip from her hands, watching it flutter to the floor, watching it settle on the rug as though it were a singularly ungainly butterfly. Then she couldn't think, she couldn't get it straight, all she understood was she had to get home, she had to confront Mike, lie to him, she had to see Peter, surround herself with that entity she called family . . . because that's where she'd be safe.

She stepped into the corridor, pulling the door quietly shut behind her. LIST OF ALL, she thought. But she hadn't read the rest of it, had she? No, there hadn't been time for any of that. It was just a form, just printed matter. It had no connection with her. She pressed the

button for the elevator. LIST OF ALL—LISTOFALL—
then it was just meaningless nonsense. She heard the
elevator rise in the shaft. It made a level humming noise.
She'd get inside. She'd go home. Everything was going to
be okay. The doors slid open. She entered. She pressed
the button for the ground floor. She closed her eyes. If
you don't think, she told herself. If you just don't think.
She pressed her hands together.

There was no wedding ring.

Oh Christ, Mike's ring. She must have left it on the
bedside table. After scooping it from under the bed she
must have laid it on the table and then forgotten it.

How could she have done something like that?

She'd have to go back up. She'd have to press the
button and make this car stop and then press another
button, but she couldn't remember the floor number now.
Nine? Ten? She stared around the elevator, as if she
might find some answer in the panelled wood. Nine, ten,
how could she tell? If all the goddam floors looked alike,
how the hell could she tell? She wanted to weep. She kept
on stabbing at the buttons, but the car was still going
down, down, and somehow she imagined that the further
down it went the faster it moved, but that couldn't be.
Control yourself, Kate. You find the apartment. You ring
the bell. You get your ring. A simple series of actions.
ABC. Nothing to it.

But why wouldn't the cab respond to her pressing the
fucking buttons? Figure it out. Simple, if you wouldn't
panic, if you'd only stop to think. Somebody has pressed
the call button on another floor. Right? The thing won't
respond to you until it's answered the prior call, right?

Right, Kate. So you wait. You try to be patient. You'll
get your ring back. She shut her eyes. When she opened
them she looked at the flashing numbers. The brown
walls—why did she allow them to press in on her like
some terrible weight? The old claustrophobia. She put a
hand to her forehead. Clammy. The car stopped. She
looked at the indicator and saw that she was on the fifth
floor. An old woman, wrapped in an ancient fur with the
head of a dead fox appended to it, stepped inside. The
doors slid shut again. Kate leaned against the wall,
waited, catching the sickening scent of camphor. She

peered at the old woman. Then the car stopped again, this time at the lobby. Moving very slowly, sighing to herself, her dentures clicking, the old woman got out. Kate pressed the button marked ten, watched the doors close, then thought: Hurry. Please hurry. The ring. That's all you want now. Don't even think of anything else. Don't think.

She stared at the numbered lights. Eight, nine, ten. Ten is right, she thought. It has to be ten. She felt the car shudder to a stop. The doors opened.

At first she couldn't understand. She thought: This is all some terrible mistake, it doesn't make any sense; you must have found the wrong person; my name is Kate, Kate Myers, please. . . . Then she was aware of something else, the motion of metal through air, the strange whispering sound, the sight of herself reflected in the dark glasses, the way she raised her hand to fend off the piece of metal, but that must have been later because she felt a sharp pain flash through her wrist and she saw blood rising from her skin. Then the metal was being raised in the air again and the doors were closing, the car was moving, the blonde woman was striking the air and the metal was flashing in the light of the car—

It was a dream, a sick dream, something you dredged up from a deep place inside yourself, your own theater of the absurd, your own auditorium of menace.

But why was the pain so fucking real?

Why did she hear herself scream so loudly?

I was looking for my ring, that was it. The wedding ring. And I couldn't find it, no matter where I looked.

Blood ran in her eyes. She put a hand up to her face. The blade fell again, slashing across her fingers. She felt herself slide down against the wall, blinded, pain piercing her with the intensity of a laser. She covered her head with her hands but the pain had moved elsewhere. She crossed her legs. She was bleeding down there, bleeding from the crotch. She tried to rise. She tried to push the blade away but she couldn't, it just kept falling and falling. She tasted her own blood. She tried to wake up, to force herself out of the nightmare—but there was no end to it. She imagined she heard the name "Elliott," but suddenly there was a great and terrifying distance between herself and the

world; it was like some harsh tide that, as it ebbed back
to the horizon, carried her away to a dark place, a dark
sun, a black sky. And still, fainter now, she could feel the
slicing of the blade.

She had the absurd thought: I'm dying.

But that couldn't be right.

That just couldn't be right.

Even as the lights faded and the sound of the blade
became no more than a breeze blowing in a spider's web,
she knew it couldn't be right.

5

Liz watched the door close, saw Ted's hand uplifted in a
coy little wave, and then she was alone in the corridor,
passing under the lamps to the elevator. He was okay, she
thought—what you'd call a nice ineffectual guy, probably
house trained and henpecked by a wife and shabbily
treated by a boss. You could read the story of his life in
his sex act—shyness, reluctance, a certain softness. He'd
probably saved up to get laid and his wife was back in a
place like Syracuse or Quincey, thinking he was on a
business trip. Maybe, she thought, the thing that glues
relationships together isn't love or affection, but some
emotional sleight of hand, a trickery of the heart, a
collection of tiny deceits and minuscule treacheries. There
was something depressing in that.

She stopped at the elevator and pressed the call button.
As she waited she looked along the empty corridor at the
wall lamps. Sometimes apartment buildings were spooky,
like all the inhabitants had upped and left. You could
imagine opening all the doors and stepping inside rooms
filled with furniture covered over by dust sheets. She
listened, hearing the motion of the elevator in the shaft.

She was dogged by tiredness again; she should have
taken the day off—but somewhere her internal calendar
was telling her about time passing, a message that became
increasingly urgent. Two years: would she look back later
and say they'd been worth it? The decision back then had
been cold and deliberate, reached out of an understanding
that the world was a hard place to be without bread and
that the most saleable commodity you possessed was your

own body. She yawned, leaned against the wall, heard the sound of the elevator growing louder.

The lights on the panel blinked. The elevator came. The doors slid open.

Later she would try to remember what she felt, she would try to remember what she saw, and at the core of the memory there would be confusion, panic, terror, and the strange constricted echo of her own scream.

THREE

1

Sometimes it seemed to Marino that the world was nothing but the sum of grief, that suffering was the major part of that entity called the human condition. The only answer maybe was to immunize yourself against it, the way some of the older cops had done, going the hard-bitten route, refusing to be surprised by anything, refusing to be disgusted by anything, hiding under a veneer of easy cynicism. It wasn't his way, even if he had tried it: he couldn't wear cynicism like it was a badge you got in return for several years of service. He had other, simpler, escapes—like having a quiet dinner with his wife in a place on Mulberry Street or taking his kids to a ball game. They were temporary releases from an aching concern; it was like Mary always said: *You get too wrapped up in all that stuff, Joseph* (always Joseph, never Joe). *Why can't you just see it as a job?*

He wondered why he couldn't, why the frequent brutalities the city threw up from its darkest places always affected him personally. You put on a front, sure, because you had to; but inside there was the feeling of an emotional meltdown. A corpse—maybe that of a young kid senselessly stabbed or a bum knifed for a half-pint of booze—any corpse always made him feel sick in his gut, always carved some hollow out of his heart. I'm soft is all, he sometimes thought. But the more he thought that the more he tried to hide the softness away, as if the simple human reaction to homicide were a terrible weakness. *Can I help what I feel?* he'd asked Mary once. She hadn't answered the question, or if she had he couldn't remember.

Now, sitting behind his desk, he closed his eyes and

54

rubbed his eyelids with the tips of his fingers. He sighed. There was a flash again of the dead woman in the elevator. I don't need that, he told himself. There had been more blood than you'd expect to find in a slaughter-house. One of the guys from the medical examiner's office had counted eighteen different incisions made by the blade of the open razor. Okay, he thought. On the bottom line you can't even imagine the most vindictive kind of vengeance needing that frenzied killing. Two fingers had been mutilated from the right hand. Between the legs the blade had laid the flesh back to the pubic bone. Three times the blade had sliced the skin around the eye, cutting the eyeball open. If I were going to kill somebody, he thought, it would be one shot from a Magnum in a dark place. But that was a rational murder—here you were dealing with something else altogether. Madness. The specific frenzy of insanity. He wondered what she'd felt when the razor first came down. Surprise? Fear? Whatever, it would boil down to the bleak understanding that your clock had run out, and that you were as alone as you had ever been. . . .

He opened his eyes, blinked against the fluorescent light overhead, glanced at the folder on his desk, then stared at the young woman who sat opposite him. Pretty. And scared to death. Watching her, he experienced a wave of weariness rush through him.

He said, "Let's run it through again."

The young woman stared at him. "Do we have to?"

Marino nodded. He leaned back in his chair, raising one finger to touch the fringe of his dark moustache. He slid his hands inside his belt and thought: I need to lose some poundage soon. I need to cast off some of this heaviness before I become a total blimp.

"You pressed the button for the elevator," Marino said.

"I did—"

"Then the car came—"

"Right. The car came."

He studied her face again. Somehow he couldn't make the connection between the face, the strange innocence of it, and the stuff he'd learned from the fact sheet that lay

in front of him. Butter would have a hard time melting in
her mouth, he thought. So much for appearances.

She was silent. She rubbed the palms of her hands
together.

"The car came," she said. "I don't remember exactly
the sequence of events."

"Try."

"I'm trying." She smiled at him. It was a forlorn little
expression, a brave front. "You don't run into a situation
like this every day, Lieutenant."

He leaned forward now. "The door opened."

"Right. The door opened. It was horrible. It was just
so goddamn unspeakably . . . " She turned her hands over
and stared at the palms. Lovely long fingers, Marino
thought.

"I *know* it was horrible," he said. "I saw it, remember?" He listened to the sound of telephones ringing in
the other offices. A shadow passed in front of the glass
door. He watched it a moment. Then he was thinking of
the husband that Sergeant Levinski had taken down to
the morgue for an ID. You could see it in his eyes, grief
struggling with the misplaced hope that it was all some
fucked-up mistake, that the corpse in the cold room
wasn't his wife after all, a stranger, somebody he'd never
seen before. Poor bastard. And then there was the kid,
sitting out there right now like a zombie, waiting for the
husband to come back from the ID. One shattered family,
for Christ's sake, and that thought hurt him, because that
was the place where you started to identify, you started to
say *it could've been my wife.* . . . He forced his mind away
from that direction.

He said, "Okay. The doors opened. You saw a woman
lying in her own blood. Then what?"

"I reached inside the elevator—"

"Why?"

"Why? Jesus, I don't know why. She was moaning. She
lifted her hand in the air. Real slow. I just reacted
instinctively. I might have screamed. I don't know."

"Then what?"

"Then I saw this other woman, a blonde with these
black glasses on, and she had this razor in her hand. She

must have pressed the button because the doors started to close. Look, I don't remember the sequence, dammit."

Marino leaned back again, his chair tilted to the wall.

"Then the woman tried to slash me with the razor—"

"While the doors were closing?"

"I guess. Anyhow, I must have pulled my hand away, then the razor fell to the floor and I picked it up—"

"That's what I'd like to know about. Why did you pick it up?"

She shook her head from side to side, opened her purse, took out a cigarette. Marino pushed a book of matches across the desk towards her.

"Maybe I thought I should defend myself. I don't know. A lot of things run through your head fast. Maybe I thought I could help the dying woman, I don't know."

"So you pick up the razor. The doors close. The car goes down."

"Right."

"And then, still holding the razor, you rush down the stairs to the lobby—"

"But she was gone when I got down. There was only the dead woman in the car, the blonde had gone. I must have been shouting something like—shit, I can't remember."

"So you're left in the lobby, holding the murder weapon, and there's no sign of the alleged killer."

"Alleged? What do you mean *alleged?*"

Marino put his elbows on the desk. His leather jacket crackled. He smiled at the woman. "You were the only person to see this tall blonde lady with the glasses, right?"

"Hey, hold it—"

"Nobody else saw her."

"I don't think I like the direction of this, Lieutenant."

"The razor has a perfect set of your prints."

"Obviously," she said, defensive now. "I picked the goddamned thing up, didn't I?"

Marino watched her in silence for a moment. "You want to know how I know they're *your* prints, Miss Blake? Or can I call you Liz?"

She reached for the matches, lit her cigarette. She blew

a stream of smoke at him. He stood up, the folder open in his hand. "Arrested January 4, 1979, act of prostitution, Park Avenue Hotel—"

"Okay," she said. "Big deal. You've got my prints on record—"

"March 19, same year, act of prostitution—"

"That was goddamn entrapment," she said. "That was some vice squad guy who used a certain escort service, and it was a bum deal that didn't go down—"

Marino closed the folder. He leaned against the wall. "Check one, your prints on the murder weapon. Two, the deceased's blood on your clothes. Three, a neat set of scratch marks from the deceased's nails across your hand—"

"Why the hell would I want to kill her? I didn't even know the woman. You can't hang this on me. No way." She stubbed her cigarette underfoot, an impatient stamping gesture. Marino stared at the sparks that fluttered up, then died.

"You're a hooker, Liz. A pretty expensive hooker, but a hooker just the same. And right now everything points in your direction, doesn't it?"

She watched him in silence. She fumbled nervously with her purse, snapping the clasp time and again. She's scared, he thought. You could almost smell the fear upon her.

"I didn't know this woman. I didn't kill her. It was pure accident, coincidence, call it what you like, that I was waiting for the elevator at that time. . . ."

Marino said, "You were in the building during the course of your business, right?"

"Look, I was visiting a friend—"

"What friend?"

"Ted. I don't remember his last name. He was from out of town. The apartment was borrowed."

"Some friend," Marino said. "Must be real close, if you don't know his last name."

She looked down at the floor for a moment, then raised her face angrily towards him. "Why the hell are you giving me such a hard time? I don't need this. Why are you putting me through this shit?"

Marino sat down again. He watched her for a while.

Putting her through the shit, he thought. He felt almost
sorry for her: a moment of weakness. Try another tack,
another direction.

"Maybe you can give me a general description of this
... alleged blonde?"

Her expression was cold. A face like that shouldn't
look so chilly, he thought. It was the kind of face that
might belong to the hostess-wife of some young hotshot
attorney angling for a partnership in his firm, giving
dinners and gracing parties with her presence, making
sure the martinis were just so, the food exactly right.
Instead, a goddamn hooker.

"The alleged blonde was maybe five-ten. Pretty tall
anyhow. I can't be exact," she said.

"Wearing what?"

"I didn't have time to look. I only remember her
face—and not too much of that because of the glasses."

"Yeah, the glasses—"

She leaned forward in her chair, her face strained.
"Look, if you think I did it, why don't you just go right
ahead and arrest me?"

"It's a temptation," Marino said.

"I get the feeling you don't believe a word I'm saying—"

Marino looked down at the surface of his desk. It wasn't
a matter of belief or disbelief; it was all a process of
elimination in the long run, striking names off lists, erasing
motives, hoping that in the end you came up with the
candidate most likely to ... He watched her now, touching his moustache lightly, wondering if his wife were
right: *That strip of hair does nothing for your face,
Joseph.* He smiled at her. "I want you to look at some
mug shots."

"Does that mean you believe me?"

Marino shrugged. He picked up the telephone, said
something into it, and a few moments later a uniformed
cop came into the office.

"Niven, take Miss Blake here and show her some mug
shots."

The uniformed cop looked at Liz, who got up slowly
and followed him to the door. Marino stood up.

"Liz," he said.

She turned round in the doorway.

"One thing," he said. "Don't leave town. I'll be keeping tabs."

She stared at him, then she left. Alone, Marino picked up a piece of paper from his desk. It was covered with his handwritten notes, scrawled words done in black ballpoint. The itinerary of a dead woman, he thought. A journey into oblivion. A trip to nowhere. The husband had said she'd gone to an appointment with her shrink, a certain Dr. Elliott. (Why a shrink? The husband hadn't been sure, but then he hadn't been in the mood to be sure of anything very much.) After that, she'd gone to the Museum of Modern Art, which was where that character Lockman had picked her up. A casual pickup, a slice of midday frivolity, some spice. (Question: Did she do that kind of thing often? Was it a one-shot deal?) He'd talked to Lockman already when he'd gone to the apartment building after the slaying—but the guy didn't even know the dead woman's name, for Christ's sake. Anyhow, he'd come forward during the commotion in the building, he'd volunteered the information about the pickup, about how the afternoon was spent, and Marino had no instinctive reason to distrust the guy. Some apartment building, he thought. Everybody's getting laid in the afternoon, it seems. He made a small cross against Lockman's name, then he pushed the paper aside and rose, standing in the doorway of his office, looking out across the collection of desks in the large central office. The sight depressed the hell out of him somehow. Maybe it was the dreary institutional color of the walls or the faded Wanted posters or the endless ringing of telephones.

Across the room, on a bench pressed to the wall, he saw Kate Myers' son. The sight touched him: he felt a vague pain, like a knot, in his throat. He wanted to go over to the kid and say something, but what the hell could you say? He was just sitting there looking forlorn, confused, empty, struggling with God knows what grief. You don't have time to bask in pity, he told himself. Who needs it?

He went back to his desk, picked up the telephone, pressed a button. "Send me Betty Luce. Yeah. Right now." When he put the receiver down he sat for a time

staring into empty fluorescent space, wondering about Liz
Blake's blonde with the black glasses, wondering about
Kate Myers' shrink, wondering in that pointless way in
which random thoughts turned over and over until they
came full circle.

He closed his eyes a moment, trying to drift away from
the noise around him, but what he saw was the butchered
woman lying in the elevator car, razored to a point that
was almost beyond recogniton.

Liz turned the stiff pages of the book of mug shots. She
couldn't stop her hand from shaking—it wasn't the flat
dead eyes of the women who stared out of the photographs that bothered her; it wasn't even the memory of
seeing the elevator doors open, the sound of her scream,
the sight of that blood-red car, the reflection of herself in
the black glasses, the cold arc of the blade whistling
through the air and missing her hand by inches, it wasn't
even the touch of the dying woman and the feel of the
fingernails scraping the back of her hand—

It was Marino. It was the idea Marino entertained
that she'd done the killing. How the hell could he
even *think* that? She turned the pages. Now she was
hardly seeing the photographs. They all looked alike, the
same grim expressionless faces: they were like the pictures of victims of some ancient war. How can he think I
did it? The bastard . . . She lit a cigarette, watched the
smoke drift and curl upwards to the dim strip of fluorescent light. She thought: A minute or two earlier, a minute
or two later, and I wouldn't have seen a goddamn thing, I
wouldn't be here now suspected of killing a woman I
never even met. She lightly rubbed the side of her head;
some tiny ache was starting there, a faint pulse. Maybe he
doesn't really think I did it, maybe he believes me. . . . But
she couldn't be sure of that, she couldn't be sure of
anything.

The blood-red car.

The touch of the dying woman.

Those black glasses.

She felt cold even though the room was stuffy, overheated. She remembered rushing down the stairs, the
razor in her hand; she remembered shouting something,

words, words, indistinct in her recollection. Why did she
run like that? Some heroic instinct? Catch the killer
coming out of the elevator in the lobby? And then there
were doors opening, other people emerging from apart-
ments: a Puerto Rican maintenance man who started
screaming in Spanish, an elderly woman who fainted—the
total confusion of death. And the sight of that poor
woman in the car, surrounded by her own blood, her face
slashed so that it resembled some hideous Halloween
mask.

She turned another page. The faces stared at her. They
were empty faces. They meant nothing to her. She gazed
at her hand, trying to still the way it trembled.

She looked up at the grimy window, the darkness of
the city pressing upon the glass.

It struck her then.

It came at her like the rush of a wild arrow.

I saw the killer.

Nobody else.

She felt dizzy. She felt a certain tightness in her chest.

I saw the killer.

I would recognize her again.

No, she thought. You wouldn't. You didn't get a long
look, only a flash, a quick flash.

But the killer didn't know that.

The killer didn't know.

She was afraid suddenly, staring at the blackness
against the glass, conscious of the overhead light humming, aware of the noises all around her, she was afraid.

Then she tried to relax. Even if the killer was scared
that I could identify her, how would she know where to
find me? The thought made her feel easy. It was a large
city: it was a city where you could easily lose yourself.
She couldn't find me even if she tried. Could she?

She sighed, seeking relaxation, ease, but it wouldn't
come.

2

Elliott picked up his telephone and dialled his home
number, imagining the ringing sound echoing in the darkened master bedroom of the house in White Plains,

imagining his wife reaching for the receiver—groggy, doped out on one of her sleeping pills, her movements slow and cumbersome. He looked across the surface of his desk as he waited: the pale bulb of the angled lamp threw a thin light down on the neat pile of folders, the flimsy copies of correspondence that hadn't yet been filed. He picked up a letter opener and turned it around in his fingers, then he found himself looking at the answering machine. He'd listened to the taped messages several times, unwilling to believe at first what he'd heard, then ready to accept it only after it had been repeated, then repeated again. Kate Myers, he thought. It couldn't be possible. But the voice was so certain, so assured, that he had to dismiss the thought that it was some wretched practical joke.

He laid the letter opener down, touched the ON button of the answering machine, and then he heard his wife answer the telephone. He pressed the OFF button, listening to the dreamy quality of her voice.

"Hello," she said, drawing it out into three syllables.

"It's me," he said.

"Oh." Then, after a pause, "What time is it?"

Elliott looked at his watch. "It's almost nine. You must've gone to sleep early."

She was silent for a time. Now he could picture her clearly, her face faintly puffy from the sleeping pills, her body spread across the bed as she held the receiver. He could see her dark hair contrasted against the white pillows, the way she held the receiver with the cord coiled around her fingers, as if she were afraid of the frailty of a telephone connection.

"I was tired," she said. "Are you all right?"

"I'm fine." He hesitated, looking at the answering machine, remembering the echo of Bobbi's voice. *I guess you found what I took, didn't you?* And then the other message, the one from the lieutenant. *One of your patients, Kate Myers, was murdered late this afternoon....* Now they ran together in his brain, the two messages playing one against the other, playing in a confused way. For a moment he couldn't think straight. How could there be a connection between poor Kate and Bobbi? How could there be? He looked at his fingers in the light of the lamp;

there were lines of sweat forming like webs between the fingers. *I'd like you to get over to the thirteenth precinct as soon as you can, Doctor.*

His wife yawned. He heard the escape of air, only partly stifled by her hand. He thought how ugly she looked when she yawned, her face distorted by the movement of mouth; it was almost as if, for a fraction of time, she had an enormous gaping hole instead of a face.

"Are you coming home tonight?" she asked.

Why? he wondered. Why did he feel a vague sense of dread? It wasn't possible that there was some connection between Bobbi and Kate. They didn't know each other. They hadn't even met, so far as he could tell. Therefore: no relationship, no connection, nothing.

The razor.

He shut his eyes. "Something has happened," he said. "One of my patients was murdered today—"

"No—"

He waited a a moment before saying, "I don't have any details yet. I saw her only this morning. I have to talk to the police tonight. . . ."

Suddenly it seemed to him that she was no longer there, that she had somehow evaporated at the other end of the line. He had the feeling of talking into an electronic nothingness, his voice whipped away from him, spilled down wires, broken into syllables, then analyzed into the most minute sounds. Then she sighed and the illusion was broken.

"You'll sleep in your office?" she asked, and there was a sad resignation in her question.

"Probably," he answered.

"I'm sorry about your patient. Really I am."

"I know." He blinked into the bulb of the lamp. He looked down at his desk. He read a part of a letter beginning, *Dear Professor Samuelson, I shall be very happy to join your symposium. . . .* "Look, if it isn't too late, I'll try to get back tonight."

She was yawning again. He imagined the great house, the empty rooms, the orderly nature of everything, the curious sense he sometimes had of an absence of life in that house—or was that an absence of love? Love, he thought. Love was a perishable commodity. It became as habitual as the act of shaving in the mornings. The thought irritated him because it stirred some odd longing inside him, as if what he hungered after more than anything was the return to some former condition when the heart was easy, the passion strong. . . .

She said, "You won't be back tonight, will you?"

"I can't promise. I'll try."

"It doesn't make much difference, does it?"

He didn't answer. He heard her light a cigarette. Then he thought of how the smell of tobacco hung in her hair, adhered to the folds of her clothing, seemed to sink into the depths of her skin. He wasn't sure why smoking repelled him the way it did. If he'd asked why, if he'd delved into the nature of the thing, it would have been like a bad joke—the analyst analyzing himself. He understood that he didn't want to be near her, he didn't want the feel of her against him, the odor of tobacco, the surface of skin against skin. Love gives way, he thought. It dies. It dies and somehow you miss the funeral, the wake, the smell of smoke from the crematorium. It dies unmourned, a hobo in a pauper's grave.

"I'll see you when I see you," she said. Click.

He held the receiver a moment longer, then he set it down; he got up from his desk and went inside the bathroom that adjoined his office. He turned on the light, looked at himself in the mirror, then washed his hands at the sink. He opened the medicine cabinet. He somehow thought the razor might be there, the theft of it some act of his imagination, but of course it wasn't there.

And Kate Myers was dead.

Momentarily he felt a wave of nausea, a warmth in the pit of his stomach. He made a cup of his hands and splashed his face with cold water. *Kate Myers dead.* It was senseless. Meaningless. He turned to the window and, with a flick of his wrist, pulled open the slats of the pale blue venetian blind; the city lay in front of him, like something that wasn't rooted in concrete but afloat in the night sky in a mad explosion of lights. He stared at the lights. A lunatic city. He found himself thinking of home —not the mausoleum of a house in White Plains, but the place he considered home—England, the Sussex Downs that swelled above Brighton, remembering long walks on wonderful summer nights, remembering how he and his wife would take one of the double-decker buses up to the Downs and then, arm-in-arm, go strolling over the soft land. That wasn't me, he thought. Someone else. Not me. He let the slats slip back into place, wanting the memories to stop, but there were faint echoes still, strains of disintegrating conversations.

Do you really want to try America? Anne asked.

It's the land of opportunity, he'd said.

I don't know if I want to be one of the huddled masses.

Huddled masses. Land of opportunity. It had been good to him too; the way had been easy, too easy. But why was there this strange emptiness? He remembered the past too vividly, those lanes that ran down to the promenade and the sight of the English Channel chopping the skyline beyond the weathered rows of white-fronted hotels, the upstairs gallery in a bar called The King and Queen where he'd sat often with Anne, the drive from Brighton to Lewes, where they'd park the car and just walk (it was always summer in his memory, always leafy, the land verdant), how they'd stop at The Swan in Falmer on the way back.

The huddled masses, he thought. Dear God. It hadn't been like that at all. He switched off the bathroom light. He took his coat down from a hook and put it on. In the outer reception room he paused, standing there in a manner that suggested he'd forgotten something. But he hadn't. There wasn't anything.

He patted the pockets of his coat, heard his keys rattle, and then he went out into the lobby. He wondered where Bobbi was now, what she was doing, and why she hated him so much.

I made a certain decision, he thought. I made a certain decision that I knew was the right one. And he dismissed from his mind the creeping possibility that he might have been wrong.

He might have been mistaken.

As he closed the front door behind him, as he walked toward the street, he thought: Kate Myers is dead.

3

The boy watched the overhead lights. He thought that if he kept staring at them he wouldn't have to *really* think, he could hide away from his innermost feelings, somehow disguise himself, create a retreat from his own sense of turmoil. But it wasn't working, it just wasn't working, because other things kept intruding and when they did he felt he wanted to cry.

But crying isn't any good, he thought. Crying doesn't help. So he squinted his eyes and looked upwards. . . .

There must have been terrible pain. . . .

No. Don't think that way.

Somebody in a uniform stopped beside him and asked if he wanted a drink. He shook his head. His throat was dry but he didn't want anything to drink. The cop went away. The boy looked across the room. There was a pretty woman of about twenty-one in an office on the other side. She was leafing through a book of some kind. A book of photographs.

Pain, she must have felt. . . .

He forced his mind elsewhere. Think of anything but her, the way she died. Anything. There are three main types of fluorescent light. Preheat. Rapid-start. What was the other one? It had slipped his mind.

He took his glasses off, rubbed the corner of an eye, put the glasses back. Preheat and rapid-start and *something else?* But what? At each end of the tube there's an electrode, a coil of tungsten coated with chemicals; the chemicals are known as rare earth oxides. A device called the ballast provides voltage to start the lamp and regulate the flow of current in the—

Somebody was sitting down beside him, a man with a leather jacket and a dark moustache that he kept touching. A cop, the boy thought: the guy in charge of finding the killer.

Terrible pain and fear . . .

The cop touched him lightly on the back of the wrist. "I'm Lieutenant Marino," he said. "You're Peter, right?"

Peter nodded. The third type was called—

"This is a nightmare," Marino said. "If there's something I can do, kid."

"Catch the killer," the boy said, surprised by the venom in his own voice.

Marino smiled in a slow sad way. "I'm trying."

Peter stared down at his satchel. From some place far inside him came a devastation, a biting chill of loss, regret, a sorrow that was irreducible to language. It came up so hard and so fast he could taste it in the back of his throat. He thought: I could have gone with her this morning. I could have gone to the museum. Then to lunch.

And none of this would have happened and I wouldn't be sitting here, sitting here trying to think of anything else in the world except that one godawful fact, her death, the way she died. . . .

"I'm really going to try," Marino said.

The boy caught a scent of some kind of deodorant mingled with sweat. He rubbed his forehead. It was so damned hot in this precinct office. Maybe somebody could open a window, turn the thermostat down, something. A current flows through the gas from electrode to electrode, forming an arc. He shut his eyes a moment against the overhead lights. Thinking electrodes won't bring her back. Thinking tungsten and argon atoms won't bring her back from wherever she is.

Both of them are dead.

It hadn't occurred to him before, and now it did with something of a start. Both of his parents were dead, which meant there was only Mike. Mike. But Mike didn't like him and he didn't like Mike. That equality, like a well-grounded formula, pleased him for a second. Then he thought what Mike would be going through at the morgue and he felt sorry for the guy.

He stared at Marino. "You got any leads?"

The cop hesitated, then shrugged. "We've got a witness, I think."

I think, Peter wondered, what was that supposed to mean?

"Who?" he asked.

"That young lady over there." Marino pointed across the desks of the central office. "She claims she saw the killer."

Peter looked over the room. The young woman was still leafing through the books, laboriously turning pages. She appeared pale, nervous, finishing one cigarette only to light another. He watched her for a time. The third kind is called instant-start. Right. He had it. He remembered it. But then the other thing intruded again, assailed him, and he had to turn his face away from the cop and shut his eyes and grit his jaw. The cop touched the sleeve of his jacket.

"Listen, I can get somebody to take you home, Peter. You don't need to wait around here."

"I'll wait," Peter said.

"Yeah. I guess your father won't be much longer."

"He's not my father," Peter said. Tears formed in his eyes. He tried to blink them away, wondering why he was betrayed by his own physical responses. "He isn't my father."

"No?" Marino looked puzzled a moment.

"He's my mother's husband. There's a difference."

"Your stepfather, then."

Peter said nothing. Stepfather seemed like a dirty word to him, like something out of a fairy tale, something soaked in a terrible cruelty. But Mike wasn't cruel, just uncaring. Just cold and distant and numb.

"You sure you don't want a Coke?" Marino asked awkwardly. "We got this ancient machine that still dispenses Cokes in bottles. You hardly ever see them like that these days. Cans, always in cans. It doesn't taste the same to me unless it comes in a bottle."

Peter understood. The cop was trying to make him feel easy, trying to divert his mind from the fact of the murder. It was a gesture, a kind one, but meaningless anyhow. Peter shook his head and said, "I'm not thirsty."

Marino got up from the bench. He patted Peter on the shoulder. *Cheer up*, that was what the touch meant. Oh, Christ, the boy thought. Sweet suffering Christ, why did this have to happen? And then the pain came up from below again, a black thing moving through him like a cancer shadow. Absently, he looked across the room, watching Marino wander from one desk to another, talking with some cops. One of them was laughing at something, a gesture, a sound, that struck Peter as being all wrong, out of place. He stared back towards the girl. She was sitting with her head in her hands now, a cigarette burning on her lips, her purse hanging from the back of her chair. No more pain, he thought. Being sad is useless.

She'd told him that once and he remembered it now. The day they knew his father had been killed in Vietnam. She'd said something like: *Try to remember him the way he was, try to remember only the good things and the terrific fun we all had; try, and you'll see that being sad is useless.* . . . He banged his hands together angrily. She's gone—and that seemed to him ludicrous somehow; in an age of interplanetary spacecraft, high-intensity lasers, computer chips with the capacity of storing 15,000 bits, requiring a density of 3.3 million bits per square centimeter, in an age like this they hadn't devised a way of bringing people back from the dead.

He opened his satchel, looked inside, closed it again. Then he sat back with his eyes shut, trying desperately not to think of anything at all, not to remember, dream, fantasize. There was just this enormous space inside himself, like a gash, a terrible wound, one you couldn't smear with first aid cream and put a plaster over, one that only time and justice could heal.

Justice. Catch a killer. He wondered how long it would take them to do that. Somewhere at the back of his mind he remembered reading about the number of unsolved homicides in the city of New York in a single year, and although he couldn't recollect it with any exactness, he remembered it was high, too high. And it nagged him to think that maybe his mother would become one of those unsolved cases, another statistic in a ledger of failure.

He gazed back at the fluorescent lights again. An electron in the arc strikes a mercury atom, raising the energy level of another electron in the atom, then you've got invisible ultraviolet rays. Invisible, he thought. Death does that too, doesn't it? It makes people invisible. He wondered remotely if there might be a spiritual life, existence on some other plane, but he wasn't willing to put any bets on it. Maybe you died and that was the end. Blackness. Nullification. Then life was pointless, wasn't it?

He wondered what his mother had believed at the very last, if she'd had the time to believe anything at all. He clasped his hands in his lap. He wanted to get up and talk to the young woman and find out what she really saw, whether she was actually a witness. But he felt some terrible lethargy now, a sensation that immobilized him. The stuffy heat of the room had something to do with it, like he was melting inside. He got up and walked to the water fountain, inclined his head, let the jet strike his skin. Then, when he looked across the room, he saw Marino talking with a man in a dark coat, a fair-haired man who had about him a kind of distinguished air, who carried himself as if he were important.

He heard Marino say, "Take a seat over there, Dr. Elliott. I'll be with you in a minute."

The fair-haired man moved towards the bench. Elliott, Peter thought. His mother's shrink. He went back to the bench just before Elliott reached it and he sat down. Elliott pulled up the legs of his pants as he sat. Peter folded his arms and leaned back, closing his eyes. Again, he tried not to think of his mother, but it was even more difficult now with Elliott sitting alongside him, because the man was a direct connection with his mother. He wondered what they'd talked about together during her appointment, what secrets she'd divulged to the psychiatrist, and this made him uncomfortable, imagining that Elliott knew all kinds of things about his mother, things he'd keep locked away, old secrets.

"Are you Kate Myers's son?"

Peter opened his eyes. He turned to look at the psychiatrist. There was an expression of concern, of pity, in the man's eyes.

"Are you?" Elliott asked.

"Yeah," Peter said.

"I think I know what you're going through. . . ." Elliott became silent for a time. Then he said, "I'm your mother's doctor. Doctor Elliott. If it would help, you can talk to me any time. Any time you like. . . ."

Peter stared at the man. "Do you know who killed her?"

"No."

"Then how can you help?"

Elliott smiled. "Death is a difficult thing to deal with, Peter. Especially something like . . ." He paused, turned his hands over, gazed at his fingers. "Later, you might need somebody to talk to, that's all."

A difficult thing to deal with, Peter thought. For a moment he imagined this to be some dream, the kind of weird out-of-shape dream you wake from covered with sweat, puzzled, astonished by your own night visions. But it wasn't. She isn't going to come through the door right now, walk over to me, smile. Not now. Not ever.

"Your mother once showed me a photograph of you," Elliott said. "You and she were very close, I understand."

He handed Peter a small white card.

He said, "Feel free to call me whenever you like."

Without looking at it, Peter stuffed the card inside his jacket. Then he watched Elliott get up as Marino came across the floor. The two men went inside an office and the door was shut. Peter realized he had never been so alone before.

4

Marino had ambivalent feelings about head doctors; they were the same kind of feelings he entertained about dentists and lawyers and general practitioners of medicine— costly evils of the kind that weren't always necessary. His wife had once gone to a psychologist at the time when she'd been pregnant with their first kid; a counsellor, she called him. For some reason she'd had the feeling that the baby wasn't going to make it, or that she was too small to carry it the full term. Normal fears, Marino had told her. Which, in a roundabout expensive way, was the same thing her counsellor had told her after a half dozen sessions or so. He wondered why it took so long to wrench a platitude from some people.

Now he looked across his desk at Elliott, who sat facing him with his hands in his lap. Soft hands, Marino thought. They were the color of cream stationery. You couldn't see this guy doing manual labor of any kind, not even something simple like tending a vegetable garden.

Elliott asked, "How did she die?"

Marino told him. He looked for some expression on the psychiatrist's face, some change, but there was nothing, as if a lifetime of listening to the sorrows of other human beings had made him impassive, immune to the violences and treacheries of the species.

"Do you know who did it?" Elliott asked.

"We've got a witness," Marino said. He stared at the glass wall of the office. He could see the shape of the kid's head, the dark hair just beyond the pane. He thought: I shouldn't have talked to him. It hurt just to look at the boy.

"What did the witness see?" Elliott asked.

"The blonde with the razor," Marino said. "She says."

"You sound as if you don't believe her," Elliott said.

"I didn't say that. Miss Blake claims she didn't get a real look because of the blonde's black glasses."

Black glasses. Blonde. A razor.

Marino leaned back in his chair, wondering for a moment if something slight, something so vague as to be imperceptible, had moved across Elliott's face. Trouble is, he thought, you read too much sometimes into an expression. A habit.

"When she left your office was she alone?" Marino asked.

Elliott nodded. "So far as I could tell. But then I didn't follow her out of my reception room."

Marino stared at the guy a moment. "What was she seeing you for?"

Elliott hesitated. "I have a confidence to protect, Lieutenant."

"Yeah, I know," Marino said. "And I've got a fucking murder to solve—"

Elliott sighed. "She was having some marital difficulties. She was troubled by recurring dreams."

Bobbi. He felt some panic rise inside him, something he had to fight against to keep down. Bobbi. How could it be?

"What kind of dreams? What kind of difficulties?" Marino asked.

"Are you married?"

"Yeah, but I don't see—"

"Kids?"

"Two sons, but I still don't see—"

"When was the last time you slept with your wife?"

"I don't see it's any of your business," Marino said.

"Which is exactly how I feel about your questions concerning Kate Myers," Elliott said.

Marino smiled. He felt a surface of sweat, a filmy sheet, across his brow. He wiped it with the palm of his hand. He said, "Okay. I take the point. But I'm not asking the questions because I've got some weird hang-up, Doctor. I've got a brutally murdered woman on my hands, and *she's* past the point of being embarrassed by anything you might tell me about her."

"I'm not accustomed to discussing my cases, *any* of my cases, with outsiders," Elliott said.

Shit, Marino thought. The brick wall. The fence. And something frosty lying behind it all. "Look, I'm a cop. I'm trying to find something out here. I'm not asking for the hell of it, you know." He looked at Elliott, remembering now other cases where shrinks had been involved, or where even some ordinary physician had played a part, and the difficulties in getting anything out of them. Blood from turnips, he thought. "I'll ask in another way, Doctor. Was she looking to get killed?"

"You mean was she suicidal?"

"Right."

"No. She wasn't."

"Why do you think she picked up this Lockman character? She didn't know him from Adam. He might have been a homicidal nut."

Elliott said nothing.

Marino, sighing, placed his hands square on the desk. He looked at his own plump fingers. "So he didn't kill her. But the next one she picked up might have—"

"Are you saying she might have *wanted* to get killed?"

Marino shook his head. "I don't know. She's cruising around for some action. She allows herself to get picked up by a total stranger. Doesn't that spell out some care-less disregard for her own safety?"

Elliott was silent again.

Marino got up from his desk. He felt frustrated. He walked to the window of the office and stared out across the darkened alley. The questions, the pulling of teeth— he wished he could make other people understand how much he was drained by the whole process. It was like lighting damp candles in a black room, seeing only a shard of light before the wick failed you again. Okay, this Elliott has some oath of confidentiality, but to Marino it seemed that the priorities were wrong. The woman is dead, goddamn it, and if Liz Blake is telling the truth then there's a loony out there, maybe ready to kill again. He turned, staring at the back of Elliott's head.

"So she runs into some psycho in an elevator," Marino said. "Is that just by some great fucking coincidence?"

"I don't know," Elliott said.

"Or is this woman waiting for Kate Myers for some reason?"

Elliott turned around, shrugged, lightly touched the tip of his chin with a finger.

"Do you know any psychos, Doctor?"

"I do some work in a clinic for the criminally insane," Elliott said.

"Could she have met one of these nuts in your office? Some kind of weirdo she turned on that followed her?"

Elliott smiled for the first time. "All my dangerously disturbed patients are confined. They don't come to my office."

"Is there any kind of chance? How about a new patient, for example? Do you always know they're nuts when you see them at first? Can you always tell?"

"You can't always tell, of course. . . ."

Marino went slowly back to his desk. He sat on the edge of it, swinging one leg back and forth. "Are you protecting a patient, Doctor?"

"No. Absolutely not."

"Isn't it possible that maybe one of your patients this morning saw Kate Myers come in, then followed her when she left? Isn't that possible?"

"I think you're going in quite the wrong direction, Lieutenant," Elliott said.

"Maybe my eyewitness should take a look at the patients you saw before Kate Myers. That way we could be sure my psycho isn't your psycho, right?"

Elliott shook his head. "I'm sorry. I have to protect—"

"Yeah, the confidentiality of your patients. I know, I know. It's a shame, because it means I'm going to have to waste some time getting a court order to check out your appointments book for this morning. Too bad we can't cooperate together a little more readily. . . ."

"You can take my word," Elliott said. "I'm not protecting *anybody.*"

"Unfortunately, I can't take anybody's word in this game, Doctor. It's hard to believe, I guess, but sometimes people don't always tell the truth."

Elliott got up. For a time he didn't move from where he stood, inclining his head slightly as if he were listening for something. Marino watched him. It was a drag to go through the form-filling process of getting a court order for the appointments book, and it probably wouldn't lead anyplace, just another vague possibility to be eliminated. He stood up and said, "I'll be in touch."

Elliott went out of the room.

Marino sat back with his eyes closed, letting his mind go momentarily blank. But what came back to him, time and again, was the sneaking, nagging feeling that he'd accomplished nothing, that there were too many holes he'd failed to fill.

His door opened. Niven stood there awkwardly in a uniform that seemed one size too small for him.

Marino looked up.

"Miss Blake didn't recognize anybody," Niven said. "What do you want me to do with her now?"

"She can go home," Marino said. He wanted to say: *We can all go home.* Instead, he shut his eyes again and leaned back in his chair, trying—as he always tried—to understand the mind of the killer. But this one was strange to him, a locked room he just didn't have a key for, a door he couldn't get to open. Eighteen different incisions, he thought.

Eighteen.

What kind of frenzy was that?

5

A police car took them home, Mike sitting hunched in the back near the window, his face bleached of color, his breathing heavy as if he might at any moment break down and sob. Peter sat close to him, wishing there was something he could say, something they might say to each other—like creating a bridge, a link, across the space of grief. He glanced at his stepfather, then he stared out of the window at the darkened city, at the neon lights that punched brilliantly colored holes through the blackness like distended stars. LEROY'S BAR & GRILL. A red sign hung in a window, advertising a beer. A couple of dark shapes stood outside, passing something between themselves. A joint maybe or a brown bag of booze. ZUM ZUM—closed for the night. Then they were passing Madison Square Garden, where the sign advertised an equestrian show. Across the way a line of cabs waited outside a hotel. Funny how in the streetlights they looked more gray than yellow, gray and ghostly. The boy shut his eyes. He heard Mike sigh, then mutter something to himself. *I don't understand, I don't understand....* And then he'd taken a handkerchief from his pocket and was holding it up to his face in a strange way, as if he wanted to keep his grief hidden.

Peter glanced again at his stepfather. For a moment he wanted to tell him what he'd heard Marino and Elliott talk about, but he knew it would hurt, it would hurt real bad.

He remembered Elliott going inside the office, the door closing. He remembered how desperately he'd wanted to hear what was said between the two men. But he didn't have anything in his satchel that would help, nothing he could press against the wall, so he'd gone to the toilet to look for a glass, only he couldn't find one—just battered dixie cups, which he knew were useless. Then he'd noticed on one of the cop's desks a dirty glass that, to judge from its appearance and smell, had contained milk several days ago. It was better than nothing, he thought. So he'd surreptitiously swiped the glass and pressed the open end of it to the wall of Marino's office—sitting in such a way,

his hand held to his head, that anybody passing would
have assumed he was dejected, depressed—but he was
listening, listening to the echoing sounds of Marino and
Elliott, not understanding all of it, not liking the bits he
did understand.

Cruising around for some action . . .

His mother! It didn't sound like his mother, more like
a stranger. . . . *Blonde with black glasses . . .*

Then something about a guy called Lockman, somebody that had just picked her up. How could she have let
that happen?

There was more stuff he couldn't catch. The acoustics
were bad, too many telephones ringing, a lot of vibration,
too many people talking around him.

Could she have met one of these nuts in your office?
Some kind of weirdo . . .
Some kind of weirdo that followed her?

After that Mike had come back and there was a cop
ready to drive them home. Now, beside him, Mike had
taken the handkerchief away from his face. He turned
towards Peter as if he wanted to say something, but his
mouth opened and closed silently. Peter looked out just
as the car was turning into the street where they lived.
The apartment buildings appeared unusually dark and
silent in the night, the lights that fell against curtained
windows muted—like the whole world is mourning, he
thought. *Some kind of weirdo.*

The car slid to a stop. Mike didn't get out immediately.
Instead he sat staring at Peter, and the boy waited for
something harsh to come from his stepfather's mouth,
recriminations, dead possibilities thrown accusingly up in
his face: *If you'd gone with her to the museum, if you'd
met her and gone to lunch, it wouldn't have happened.*
But there was nothing. Only a hollow expression on the
man's face, pale as the color of the handkerchief that lay
in his fist like some huge crumpled flower.

6

Elliott switched on his desk lamp and sat down, gazing at
the surface of the desk, not really seeing what lay there,
not noticing the red light of his answering machine. It was

wrong, he thought, wrong not to tell Marino about Bobbi, but even now he couldn't make the connection between Bobbi and Kate Myers, as if the relationship were one last hurdle he wasn't prepared to leap.

How could he fail not to make it?

A razor. A tall woman, blonde hair, black glasses.

Wearily, he rubbed the side of his jaw, then he rose and crossed the floor to the window, which he pushed open. The night air was chill, refreshing, cleansing his damp skin. He looked at the sweat on his fingers. Wrong, he thought again, even under the circumstances of confidentiality, even given that ethical protection. A priest, he wondered, what would a priest do with a killer in his confessional? He wouldn't talk. The same standards applied, didn't they?

He raised his hand to the windowpane, conscious of a vague tremor in his fingers. One couldn't imagine such an event, such a tragic occurrence as that of Kate Myers dying under the savagery of an attack; nor could one imagine Bobbi doing it. He wondered if Marino had noticed anything, if some vague facial expression had given him away. Wrong, he thought. Was it wrong?

He shook his head. He turned from the window and, taking a key from his pocket, opened a case under the bookshelf. Inside there was stacked a series of tapes. He flipped through them quickly, found the one he wanted then went to his casette machine and put it on. He pressed the fast-forward button, stopped it, then punched the PLAY key. The voice was garbled, indistinct, broken by sobbing and sighing. He leaned against the edge of his desk, listening. There was something eery about hearing it now in this half-lit office in a silent building. It was almost as if he expected the door of the reception room to open, then footsteps, then Bobbi standing in the doorway. . . .

I don't know what I ever did to you, I never did anything to you, I mean, maybe you just don't give a shit, is that it, Elliott? Maybe . . . you don't care about anything, maybe there isn't a goddamn thing inside you that resembles anything human and kind. . . . I asked you . . . how many times did I . . . beg you. . . ? You can't count the times, then those nights when I wanted to die because you

*always refused me. . . . You don't know what I go through,
nothing in all your goddamn books gives you any idea,
does it? Nothing you read or hear lets you know what this
kind of fucking hell is like, Elliott. . . . I can't keep begging
and begging. . . . I don't have any fucking dignity left. . . .
You know what I think of you, Elliott? You know what
name I call you . . . ?*

He pressed the STOP button. He tried to close the
hysteria of the voice out of his mind. I did right, he
thought. I did the correct damn thing. I didn't make a
mistake. He moved away from the desk, crossed the floor,
rubbed the palms of his hands together. He heard some
inner voice contradicting him now: You did wrong, Elliott, on two counts. You denied Bobbi what she wanted.
Then you denied Marino his information. What does that
make you?

No, he thought.

Close your eyes. It goes away. You can make it go
away.

Trembling, he picked up his address file. Somewhere
there had to be a number for Bobbi. He couldn't find it.
Why couldn't he find it? Damn. He pushed the file aside.

What are you? On the same level as a priest?

He pinched the skin at the top of his nose tightly.

A headache. Nervous tension.

He went into the bathroom. He found some Equanil in
the medicine cabinet, swallowed two, lidded the bottle
and put it back. They'd help for a time. . . .

Help what? he wondered.

Help ease your feeling that Kate Myers died because of
one of your patients? Because you *failed* that patient?

No.

Some other way.

He sat behind his desk. I could call Marino, he
thought.

I could tell him I'm holding something back.

You don't know that for sure, do you?

You'd have to be blind *not* to know.

He leaned back in his chair. The room, the shadowy
bookshelves, and the pale light from the lamp and the
faint glow of the leather sofa, the room pressed in on him.

He sighed. Kate didn't die because of me. Didn't die because I made a bad decision about Bobbi. *Didn't.*

But the accusing inner voice wasn't going to be silenced easily. Now it seemed like the harsh ticking of some old clock inside him, reverberating in the skull, vibrating along the bone. You didn't help Bobbi. You should have helped Bobbi. Now Kate is dead.

He stared at the red light on the answering machine, reached forward, pressed the playback button. *Beep.* Doctor Elliott? This is Franklyn Harris, I'm stuck in Chicago, I can't make our appointment tomorrow.... *Beep.* This is Anne ... I didn't mean to be so abrupt before. Calling to say I'm sorry. *Beep.* But the tape was silent after that. Anne's English accent stuck in his mind, an accent of the South Coast, the Home Counties, smoothed and polished and precise in its vowel sounds. He reached for the telephone, picked it up, began to punch out his home number. Then he stopped and dropped the receiver back in place.

No message from Bobbi, he thought.

No gloating insane message from her.

Like what I did with your razor, shrink?

He leaned back in his chair, rocking slightly. He knew that she would call, sooner or later she'd come through, sooner or later he'd hear that deranged voice laughing at him. He put his hand up to his forehead. Perspiration. A touch of pain. How could I tell Marino? he wondered. How could I do that?

He rose, walked to the bookshelf, picked up the Manhattan Yellow Pages. He flicked through them to the section he wanted, running his finger down the page.... There was only one Levy listed as practising psychiatry in Manhattan. He wrote the address down in his notebook, closed the book. Tomorrow morning, he thought. Tomorrow morning he would go and see Levy about Bobbi.

And say what?

Say what exactly?

He wasn't sure.

He went over to the sofa and sat down. Fatigue coursed through him, a sense of impending dark, but he knew he wouldn't find sleep an easy thing.

He knew, too, that it would be filled with dreams, dreams as involuntary as muscular spasms. The last thought he was conscious of, the last flicker that went through his mind, was the question of how far and how long you could protect a patient.

He didn't know the answer.

FOUR

1

She had changed her clothes, but somehow she felt that the dead woman's blood clung to her still, that even as she sat in the bar holding a glass of scotch between her hands other people could see stains on her. But that was stupid, she thought. Nobody saw anything. Nobody could. Even if there were still stains, it was too dark, too dim, for anybody to see anything. She sipped the scotch and smoked a cigarette, trying to relax. She told herself: Don't spoil things. Don't even think of Elliott now. He would be in deep trouble soon enough. . . .

She turned her head, tossing her hair lightly, and looked around the darkened room. Only last night she'd sat here with Walter, but why did it seem so long ago now? Walter was probably back in Pocatello by this time. She finished her drink, called for the bartender, ordered a second. There was a dryness at the back of her throat, but she wasn't nervous the way she had been last night. Funny the way things change, she thought.

And yet something bothered her.

It was a small thing; it was like a piece of lint at the back of her mind. Like a faint distortion in a mirror.

She smiled to herself.

How easy it had been, how utterly simple to destroy, how weirdly fascinating to watch the way the razor had slipped through the folds of skin, slashing to bone, to sinew, slicing through the tuft of pubic hair in one wild downward swing. (No underwear. The cunt had no underwear.) A certain look in the eye, one of some inconceivable misunderstanding, one that turned to disbelief, then to pain, fear, and finally emptiness. She thought of that emptiness now. She thought of Elliott missing his razor. What will you tell the cops? she wondered. What will you say to them, shithead? Dipstick asshole. No. She'd promised herself. *No Elliott.*

She swayed her head slightly in time to the music from the jukebox. From the corner of her eye she was conscious of a man moving across the floor towards her, but she was mistaken, because as soon as he'd come level with her he went right past. She turned, seeing him go through the door to the street, trailing behind him some kind of scent, an after-shave, a cologne. She sipped the scotch, marvelling at the easy confidence the drink gave you.

It still bothered her, though. She thought: Don't let it.

It doesn't matter, whatever it is.

She closed her eyes and listened to the singer's voice. She liked the tune, the clear quality of the voice. It seemed to wrap itself around her, a certain optimism, a clarity that suggested you could hope, that hope had some meaning. She wanted to lose herself in the song, wanted to feel the atoms of herself dissolve in the notes, the tiny beats between the words of the lyric.

Don't let the other thing touch you now. It shouldn't trouble you.

She opened her eyes, seeing a reflection of herself in the mirror behind the bar. She looked, in that flattering glass, almost beautiful. And then another image moved directly behind her, the shape of a tall man, a heavy shadow. She watched his thick fingers come down on the bar beside her glass and she was reminded of the flight of a bird, a graceless bird.

"Need that freshened up?" he asked.

It was a long time before she turned around to look at him; the record changed, another took its place, and still she didn't say anything, didn't move. You have this confidence now, she thought. You have this sense of yourself soaring in some way. She leaned back slowly from her stool.

"Are you buying?" she asked.

"Sure," the man said. "If you want me to."

"Thanks."

She watched another scotch being placed in front of her by the barman. "Jackson Irving," the man said.

"Bobbi."

"Good to meet you, Bobbi."

She smiled at him, lowering her eyes a little. She wanted to taste the clichés in her mouth, run them through her head as if they were minuscule drops of sparkling water. *Do you come here often? What kind of work do you do? Do you live alone?* She wanted to enjoy these things, even if she knew they were banal, mundane, like the questions in some absurdly simple crossword.

"Live round here?" he asked. He had a moustache that reminded her of a zoo animal; she couldn't think which one. A walrus? He had glasses with thick lenses and he wore a dark suit, a handkerchief tucked in the breast pocket. He seemed strangely stiff to her, as if the clothes he wore were a starched uniform.

She nodded. "Close," she said.

She reached out and touched his handkerchief, wrecking its triangular shape. "Let me guess," she said, throwing her head back slightly, running her tongue over her lipstick, astonished by the quickening of her own confidence and how easy it was to drift into it. "You're a salesman from Greensboro."

He laughed and said, "Hell, no."

"Raleigh then."

"No."

"You mean I'm wrong?" Wide-eyed.

"I fix computers," he said.

"Is that what you're doing in New York? Fixing somebody's computer?"

He shook his head. "The company has this course every so often for its technicians. Like a refresher course. Things change so fast in the field."

She sipped her drink. Floating out, floating away; why couldn't it always feel like this? This place where there weren't any misgivings, where the uneasiness ceased to exist? A high cloud and you're strolling through it and it's light as the feather of a goose. . . .

"I'm from Watertown. Upstate New York."

"They have *computers* in Watertown?"

"Sure they do."

She laughed, leaning forward so that her face came in contact with his shoulder. Jackson Irving from Watertown was just as silly as Walter Pidgeon from Pocatello, just as silly, as charming. What did this bar have—a monopoly on hicks? He reached for his drink, a yellowy concoction on the surface of which, like a drunk's eye, there floated a cherry.

"I've never been in this bar before," he said.

"I come all the time, *all* the time." She was conscious of her own raised voice, wondering if she were talking too loudly, the sound too shrill. But Jackson Irving didn't seem to notice or care. She turned away from him for a moment, looking around the room. Near the jukebox a few couples were shuffling around in a desultory way, creating the illusion of immobility, as if what they were doing was less a dance than a process of sleepwalking. They seemed bonded together by an adhesive that couldn't be worked loose.

"Do you want to dance?" he was asking.

"I don't think . . ." She turned her face towards him. He looked so solemn, so nervous somehow, that she wanted to laugh.

"I don't dance well," he said. "I'm pretty clumsy."

"I'll risk it," she said. Why not? What was there to lose?

She got down from the stool and walked across the floor. She felt his arms go round her waist and she closed her eyes tightly. Sometimes she could feel his breath upon her skin, against the side of her neck or upon the surface of her eyelids. Let this go on, she thought. Why should the music have to stop anyhow? Why should night turn into blistering day and light rip through the fabric of everything? She shifted against him, her hip to his. She realized with some slight thrill that he was hard, the hardness pressed to her outer thigh. She opened her eyes and looked at him but he had his shut, and she was reminded of a schoolboy holding off the last stroke of masturbation, sustaining the moment. She thought: I want to be promiscuous, I want to fuck all men. . . .

Then it moved in her mind again.

The elevator. The razor dropping. That other woman reaching down and picking the razor up as the doors closed. It moved the way a dream will, disintegrating even as you think about it.

She didn't want it now. Close that door. But she remembered running, her feet clattering along a corridor, a back entrance and then an alley and then another street. It was vague and misty, an old recollection, and she didn't want it now. She pressed her face close to the man's neck. She was thinking of Levy next, trying to remember something Levy had said to her, words of comfort, promising words: *I think we can work this problem out between us.*

Suddenly she realized it was ambiguous.

We can work this problem out between us.

What was that supposed to mean?

She clasped the man tighter against her. She had to hold on to him because all at once there was an abrupt sense of slipping, as though something were breaking inside her, a euphoria yielding to a perilous dizziness, a height from which she didn't want to fall. (There were boys in the boarding school and games of rugby and the open showers after that, the boys screaming and whistling and making masturbatory gestures under soapsuds, those boys, those boys with their pale buttocks and outgrowths of pubic hair. . . . Why did she think of that now? It was somebody else's thought, a disembodied perception, unrelated to her.)

The music stopped. Jackson Irving led her to an empty booth in the far corner of the room, a dim corner where no light fell. I don't want to be here, she thought. Not now.

He sat very close to her, his hand upon the back of her wrist. He was opening and closing his mouth, words falling out like chips of sound, but she didn't understand them. She felt his fingertips slide up her bare arm and, then beneath the table, his knuckles rest upon her kneebone. She felt curiously tiny, distanced from herself, a speck floating through the dark space and back towards the light.

"What's the matter, Bobbi?"

A pulse in her throat. Something trapped there. Something trapped and dying. She wanted to cry.

"Hey, hey . . ."

She laid her head back against the leather surface of

the booth. She shut her eyes. The jukebox changed. She could hear the slow dancers shuffle still. The scraping of feet, the noise of a singer: they became one screaming sound in her head. His knuckles weren't there any more. He had turned his hand over. His palm was stroking the inside of her thigh. She opened her eyes and she thought: Everybody in this bar is watching, staring at me, at this scene going on, laughing about the hand under the table. . . .

No, nobody is. Nobody can see. Only me.

She tried to change the position of her leg but the grip against her thigh had become firm.

"Relax, relax, relax."

She stared at him. His face reminded her now of some puffy moon, the lenses of his glasses like dark craters gouged from the surface.

Cocktease is that it?

She shook her head. The grip of his hand seemed to her like the nerve center, the heart, of her sense of panic. She tried to pull herself away, but he was laughing and holding on.

And then it happened.

She saw him get up quickly from the table, his expression one of anger, his hand uplifted as if he meant to strike her. The fist hovered in the air, menacing and yet not, threatening and somehow absurd. He lowered his hand after a moment and, with a gesture of hopeless annoyance, swept her purse off the table. She reached down, fumbling for the damn thing, trying to pick up whatever had fallen out on the dark floor. She gathered it up quickly and rose and rushed towards the door and then the cold street outside.

She felt humiliated, pained, betrayed by herself.

And angry.

It was the anger that was the worst part.

She moved along the sidewalk, not thinking, not wanting to think. Wanting to hide, scream, cry, wishing a crack would develop in the universe, one goddamn hole into which she could disappear.

But the anger wouldn't go away.

It burned inside her with the intensity of molten metal.

Somehow she found a cab, got inside, told the driver just to cruise around for a time.

Touched me, she thought. He touched me.

(The air was filled with the screaming of kids, sunlight burned the grass, there were elongated shadows of trees, flattened outlines of branches etched in the grass, from somewhere the smell of a bonfire of dead leaves crackling in the long autumnal afternoon. . . .

She gazed out of the window.

Anger, hatred. Oh, Jesus.

Then she was remembering the face of the woman who'd reached inside the elevator. A pretty face. A face somebody like Jackson Irving wouldn't want to hurt, wouldn't raise his fist against. She took a Kleenex from her purse and raised it to her mouth. She was shaking. She hated herself for being so . . . so what?

Weak?

So angry?

She looked through the window at the street. It comes back, forever, to Elliott. It always comes back to him. It stops there, no matter how hard you try to prevent it. Street signs floated past like they weren't anchored to the ground, storefronts with their gridlike patterns of metal against the windows, people moving furtively through the night. The razor, she thought. But she didn't have it now.

That other woman had picked it up.

That other woman who *saw* . . .

The pretty one.

Anger is close to fear, she thought. Like two countries with a common border, a frontier you could easily pass over. Damn, that was something of *his,* something *he'd* said once, and now she was remembering in such a way that it seemed like her own thoughts. *You're angry, you're also afraid, Bobbi. When you've got a passport for one, never forget you have a visa for the other*. A visa, a passport—that was just so goddamn stupid, so goddamn banal the way he talked, the images he formed, the look on his face that made you think: He's astonished by his cleverness, the prick.

Oh Christ.

She tried to force her mind to something else, away

from Elliott. It was the young woman's face she saw, floating into her thoughts with the consistency of a nightmare.

Try to remember.

Try to remember where. . . .

Outside the window the city floated past, hewn out of the darkness like a shapeless sculpting, hacked out of the night as if some careless artist had worked out his own nightmare in concrete. She shivered, afraid now. Afraid of herself, of what she would do next.

She leaned forward and tapped the glass that separated her from the driver.

2

"I saw a *fucking murder!*"

"You've got to be kidding."

"Yeah, I'm kidding. I'm kidding so hard that the best part I've saved to the last, Norma. The cops have this weird notion I did it."

"Now I know you're joking."

"You can hear it in my voice, right?"

A pause. "You're serious, aren't you? Tell me you're not."

"I've never been so goddamn serious."

"Jesus Christ."

"I'm not sure *he* can help, Norma."

"Listen. You want me to come over?"

"I think I'd like that."

"Give me about thirty minutes."

Liz put the telephone down and walked around her bedroom. She folded her arms under her breasts. Some things, she thought, you just don't want to remember. Some things you relegate to oblivion. She went to the window and parted the curtains, looking down into the black street below. Some things you just can't put away like that, because it isn't easy. As long as you live, kid, you aren't going to forget what you saw, you aren't going to forget the blood, the sight of two faces—the victim and the assassin. No way.

She stepped out of the bedroom into her living room.

She lit a cigarette. She was cold suddenly, as if some invisible draft had rushed through the apartment. Maybe what you could do was make it seem like a dream.... The hell you could. Dreams had fuzzy edges sometimes, but this picture was outlined in black, sharp around the margins. That face behind those black glasses. She couldn't think which was worse: looking at the dying woman or staring straight at the killer.

She gazed at the scratch marks on the back of her hand.

The dead woman's last testament.

Liz strolled idly into the kitchen. She felt strangely alone in the apartment—not the sense of solitude she so often looked forward to, but something deeper and more forlorn than that. She sat down at the kitchen table. She put her hands inside the pockets of her dressing gown. Why hadn't that guy Ted come with her as far as the elevator? A simple courtesy, that was all: I'll walk you to the elevator, honey. Then she would have had a witness. But Ted, after the act, seemed only interested in her departure; like a lot of guys, a vague sense of shame accompanied detumescence. It was as if they suddenly started to remember their wives, their kids, as if they half-expected to be caught in the act. Big guilt trips. If only he'd walked to the elevator....

But no deal.

Okay, she thought. About this time I should be going into a state of shock. Instead, she felt numb and tired. She yawned, stubbed her cigarette, lit a fresh one. What kind of world was it when the employees of a so-called escort service needed to be escorted themselves? She got up and walked around the kitchen, switched on the garbage disposal, listened to the violence of the blades, switched it off again, looked inside the refrigerator, then closed the slats of the blind.

The sound of her phone ringing was startling, like the needle of some vicious dentist baring a nerve. She picked it up. It clicked, went dead.

She held the receiver, set it down, and thought: Out there in the naked city there were loonies who made these pointless calls. They wanted to irritate you. I should get an unlisted number, she said to herself. How many times had the telephone rung in the past and there wasn't anybody on the line?

A few times, she thought.

Not all that often.

Okay, so some weirdo decided to spook you with a call. Maybe a burglar checking out possible clientele. . . . Somehow this didn't convince her. She wanted to talk herself into believing it.

She picked up the receiver and dialled a number with the area code 312. She could see her mother getting up from her late-night show; she had this strange fondness for Randolph Scott movies.

"Ma," Liz said. "Did I wake you?"

"Liz? No, of course not, I was watching the box—"

"Ma, did you call me a moment ago?"

"It's funny you should ask. I was thinking of doing just that."

Telephonic telepathy. "But you didn't actually dial, did you?"

"No. Why? Somebody call you?"

Liz was silent for a second. "I guess it was nothing. How are you anyhow?"

"I'm fine. Arganbright put me on some new medication, it seems to help. At least, I don't feel quite so stiff, and the pain is less than it was."

Arganbright, the old family physician. Liz tried to picture his weary face; it was the kind of face you could imagine presiding over the deliveries of a million babies, knotting a million umbilical cords. Arganbright had even delivered her.

"Is something wrong, Liz?"

Ah. The mother's intuition. It was as eery as radar. "Nothing," Liz said.

"You're still coming at Christmas?"

"Sure I am. Looking forward to it." Like hell. The family gathering, turkey stuffing and cranberry sauce and assorted relatives, none of whom had much in common with one another, all of whom had travelled great distances for the dubious privilege of unwrapping some tinselly items and getting indigestion.

"Uncle Frank is coming," Liz's mother said.

"I'm glad to hear it." Uncle Frank, Liz thought. You could look at some old guys and just imagine them dandling seven-year-old girls lasciviously on their knees. Like Uncle Frank.

"Well, he's coming all the way from Albuquerque."

"Yeah, that's quite a trip—"

"At his age it is."

Her mother paused and Liz thought she heard the moist clicking of dentures slipping from gums.

"Your brother will be here, of course."

She thought of Ronald and his dumpy little wife. She thought of the box they called home, located in a street of underdeveloped tract houses in Phoenix. Ronald was in electronics. His little wife, Rhonda—Rhonda yet—was a part-time nurse in a local old-age home. She couldn't stand the thought of talking to Ronald, the way they chatted around the edges of threadbare memories, items from the past that Liz sometimes couldn't recall. And Rhonda would sit there with a heap of embroidery on her thick legs. My flesh and blood, Liz thought; you could work up quite a nice guilt for yourself like this, wondering why you had so little in common with your family. She entertained a supreme fantasy of sitting down to Christmas dinner and, immediately after grace, announcing the true nature of her profession. Trauma. Shock. Incredulity. *Yeah, really, I fuck for a living. It's only on a short-term basis, you understand.*

"Liz, are you sure nothing is wrong?"

"Absolutely."

"I mean, if anything *was* wrong, you'd say—wouldn't you?"

Liz recognized the tone; it was getting close to the *I-wish-your-father-was-still-alive* trip. "Ma, of course I'd tell you. But nothing is. Everything's just dandy." Dandy, she thought. That was a word you could throw in for your mother. "Look, I just wanted to call, say hello. I'll write in the next few days. Do you ... I mean, do you need anything?"

She never did; or if she did, she was too self-sufficient to ask. "All I need from you, Liz Blake, is a long letter now and again."

"You've got it."

"Take care, you hear?"

"I promise. Good night, Ma."

Liz put the receiver down.

Everything's just dandy—like being suspected of a murder.

She walked back inside the living room. She lay down on the sofa. The important thing, she told herself, is to believe in your innocence, in the fact you had nothing to do with the whole damn mess, so if they wired you up to a lie detector along the way, you'd come through with flying colors. I didn't do it, I didn't do it, she said to herself. The hell with Marino and what he might assume.

She closed her eyes. Sleepy. Weary.

She wondered about the telephone ringing. The click on the end of the line. You're safe, Liz. The killer can't touch you. You're sitting pretty.

It doesn't cut it, she thought. She sat upright. How come, if you're so safe, you feel so goddamn on edge? Norma would be here soon; some company would help, maybe even a glass of wine and a shot at sleeping. She suddenly thought of her father; it was weird and unpleasant, but she had the curious feeling at times that he was watching her, from a point beyond the grave, from someplace on the other side of death, he was watching what she was doing. And he was sick with disapproval. *Not my girl, not my little girl.* . . . She supposed this spiritualist fantasy had its roots in some guilt. She wished guilt, like dust, could be swept beneath a rug. But sometimes she felt he was up there, drifting through the clouds, shaking his bald head in sorrow.

You're being ridiculous now, she thought.

All you really remember of him is the smell of tobacco in his clothes, the way light reflected from his hairless scalp, the fact he was never short of a dollar when you badly needed anything. *There you go,* her mother would say, *always running to Daddy, Daddy's little girl.* . . . Inexplicably she felt sad; the last time she'd seen him was the day he died in the hospital, wired up to some terrible machine, his cancerous breathing coming in broken wheezes and his eyes filled with the humiliation of pain. She'd overheard one of the interns say: *That guy's got more cancer than a lab rat. You name a place, he's got it there.*

Life and love: to a ten-year-old girl these things seemed so fragile, so tenuous. When he died she remembered feeling glad he wasn't in pain any more. A sense of relief, like sunlight bursting into a room that has been shuttered way too long.

She rose from the sofa. She picked her watch up from the coffee table. It was exactly one o'clock in the morning.

3

When she got out of the cab she walked a couple of blocks, passing shuttered stores whose windows were cluttered with cameras and calculators and electronic games, passing a jazz club from whose open doors the sound of a solo saxophone drifted out in a discordant manner, a pawnshop where a dark figure lay sleeping in the doorway. She reached a corner, paused, watched a cop car cruising past in a stream of taxis; she was reminded of a dark tropical fish caught in a school of yellow ones, an outsider, one who did not belong to the fraternity. She crossed against a DON'T WALK sign, reached the other side, moved past a couple of guys arguing outside a telephone booth. Then the next block was empty, desolate, apart from herself; you might imagine the city as some void, a place of absences.

At the end of the block there was a sudden flood of light. It came from the window of a clothes store. She stopped outside and looked at the mannequins that, frozen under a blinding stream of light, suggested the newly dead. It was a bridal scene. The female stood in a cascade of white, clutching plastic flowers. The groom wore a velvet tuxedo and a red cummerbund and a shirt with lace frills. A bride and groom, she thought. A marriage of mannequins. Something about the scene reminded her—of what, for God's sake? She couldn't think. She stared into the blind eyes of the bride. Passionless, frigid. The quality of lifelessness frightened her. She tried to imagine some lewd window dresser taking their clothes off after the display had run its course, undressing them and carefully laying the man on top of the woman in a back room of the store, a dead honeymoon played out amongst the cartons and cardboard boxes of a stockroom.

She turned away, moving faster now.

The darkness around her was a chill thing. She turned up the collar of her coat. She listened to the flat echoes of her own steps as she hurried. The cold seemed to pierce the fabric of her clothing, getting down through the layers of her skin, through her nerve ends, to the surface of bone. When she reached the apartment building, she was looking for she went inside quickly, finding herself in an overheated entranceway, a floor of black and white tiles underfoot, like a vast chessboard stretching endlessly under the subdued lights.

Ahead she saw the doors of elevators.

She hesitated. She felt disoriented suddenly, lost in this place. She stopped, leaned against the wall, stared at the rows of locked mailboxes in front of her. A name, an apartment number. It doesn't matter, does it? Why does it matter?

Sixty-three. Apartment sixty-three.

She walked towards the elevators. As she did so the doors of the building swung open behind her and she turned to see a young black woman come inside—sharply dressed in a long coat with a fur trim, long brown boots, her hair braided into thin strands through which you could see the purple of her skull. She was moving towards the elevators, the heels of the boots clicking on the tiles.

The black glasses. She wanted to put on the black glasses.

She fumbled inside her purse, couldn't find them, couldn't find her protection, her camouflage. You don't need them now, she told herself. She watched the elevator doors open and she stepped inside, then she heard the black woman call out. "Hold that, will you?"

Before she could press the button for the sixth floor the black woman rushed inside the car, laughed, slumped against the wall out of breath.

"Thanks," she was saying.

Bobbi looked down at the floor, averting her face, half-smiling from some habit of politeness.

"These are the *slowest* elevators," the woman said.

Bobbie said nothing. She could feel the vibration of the car as it shuddered upwards, as if it were fighting an impossible battle with gravity. The black woman was looking inside her purse for something. She took out a Kleenex, wiped the tip of her nose, sniffed.

She hadn't pressed a button, Bobbi thought.

She was going to the sixth floor too.

If she wasn't, why hadn't she pressed a button?

She glanced at the black woman, watching the strands of hair shine, the gloss of pink lipstick. Then she was conscious of being assessed in some way, the other woman's eyes seemingly scrutinizing her. It was a quick thing, a brief look, but Bobbi caught it and wondered: Is something wrong with me? Do I look strange somehow? You imagine it, that's all. There's nothing out of place. Not a damn thing.

The car stopped and the doors slid open. She let the black woman get out in front of her. She hesitated next, watching the woman go quickly along the carpeted corridor—soundless, moving as if she weren't touching the floor. Bobbi opened her purse, pretended to be searching for something. She was aware, without looking, of the other woman stopping along the corridor and turning her face round, like she was checking to see what Bobbi was doing. But that was stupid—why should she be checking? Bobbi walked forward. Pretty soon she'll disappear, she thought. Pretty soon she'll go inside her apartment and then I won't have anything to fear. . . .

There isn't anything to fear anyway, is there?

She felt her muscles tighten, her hands stiffen around her purse. She wished she hadn't dropped the razor. She wished she had it now. She could use it. . . .

She saw the other woman pause along the corridor, ring a bell, wait. Bobbi stepped close to the wall. She saw a door open. She watched the woman go inside, then the door was closed.

The corridor was empty.

She experienced a strange falling sensation, something like panic, like the sinking of her blood, a weight dropping through her body.

No—

Quickly, she moved along the corridor.

No.

It was true. True. Bobbi put her hand up to the small wooden numbers nailed to the door of the apartment.

Sixty-three.

Why had the black woman gone inside that apartment?

She stepped back, staring at the two numbers as if they were accusing her of something. She closed her eyes tightly and bit her lip, tasting lipstick, not sure if it wasn't the taste of her own blood, if she'd punctured the surface of the lip with her teeth.

Why? For Christ's sake, why?

She turned away, filled with a sensation that was confusing, vague, as if disappointment and relief were present at one and the same time. She went back towards the elevator, pressed a button for the car, got inside when it came.

As it sank towards the lobby she wondered: How would I have killed her anyway? With what? My bare hands?

When she got out of the elevator, when she left the building and felt the cold of the night air rush through her, she realized her chance would come again. It would have to.

4

Norma had a joint in her purse which she lit as soon as she entered the apartment, taking a drag on it and offering it to Liz, who shook her head.

"Hey, it'll help you relax," Norma said.

"It's okay," Liz said. She looked at her friend for a moment. It was a godawful realization that although she had a number of acquaintances, only Norma could be counted as a real friend. "Listen, thanks for coming over."

"No sweat," Norma said. She took off her coat and sat down on the sofa. She smoked some more of the joint, then she stubbed it neatly in the ashtray. "So you really saw this killing?"

"Yeah, I really saw it."

"That's heavy."

"It's more than heavy," Liz said. "I mean, when you expect an elevator you don't expect a bloody assassination."

Norma nodded. She tilted her head back against the sofa, crossing her long legs. "What did the killer look like?"

"It's damn hard to say. Tall. Blonde. Black glasses—she had these shades that made it impossible to really *see* her face."

Norma sat forward. The whites of her eyes were faintly bloodshot now. "You want to hear something funny?"

"I'm dying to—"

"I just rode up in the elevator with a tall blonde lady—"

Liz stared at her friend a moment.

"Hey, relax. She didn't have no black glasses, though."

"What floor did she get off at? Did you see?"

"You're really uptight, honey. She got off at this floor."

"*This* floor?"

"Yeah."

Liz walked around the room, her hands in the pockets of her dressing gown. "You're kidding me," she said.

"No way. You don't think it's the same lady, do you?"

Liz shrugged. "No, I don't think it could be."

"Damn right it couldn't be. Like how could she find you? How could she know where you're at?"

"She couldn't," Liz said. It sounded unconvincing, even to her. You happen on to an event in a random way—a terrible event, but random, accidental—and there was no way the killer could know her, know where she lived. Just the same, she felt uneasy. "Can you sleep here tonight?" she asked.

"I can sleep anywhere," Norma said. "I'd like a drink. What can you offer?"

"Some wine. I think maybe there's scotch. Help yourself."

Norma went out into the kitchen. Alone, Liz stepped

towards the window, reached for the drape to pull it back—but she didn't want to look out into the street. She thought: I've never seen anybody getting off at this floor that looked anything like the woman Norma described. But that didn't mean much, not in an anonymous apartment building, not in a place where tenants came and went with restless frequency. I'm safe, she thought. I'm perfectly safe.

Norma came back with a glass of red wine. She put her hand lightly on Liz's shoulder as she went towards the sofa.

"Nothing's gonna happen, Liz—"

"Then there's the cops—"

"Listen to old Norma, huh? Them cops got nothing on you. They're playing games. Like they always play games. You know that."

"Yeah. I guess you're right."

"Sure I'm right."

There was a silence between them for a time, then Norma said, "I can sleep right here. On this sofa."

"You sure you don't mind?"

Norma shook her head. "For you, I don't mind."

Liz sat down in an armchair facing the other woman. She had a sudden flash of the scene in the elevator. It came at her, in all its terrible detail, and she tried to force it out of her mind. A thing like that, she thought, it stays with you forever.

She went over to the sofa and she hugged Norma briefly.

"Thanks. I appreciate this," she said.

"You're trembling," Norma said.

"I'm trying not to."

"You got any sleeping pills or downers?"

"Yeah."

"Take one."

"Maybe you're right."

"Doctor's orders," Norma said.

Liz went into the bathroom and opened the medicine cabinet. She removed a bottle of Placidyl, swallowed one of the capsules with some water, and then she returned to the living room to wait for sleep.

She hoped it would be dense and black and dreamless when it came.

5

Peter rubbed his eyes. He looked up from his worktable and glanced at the clock beside the bed. Normally, he paid no attention to time but now he had a feeling or urgency, an awareness of minutes passing. 3:22. How could it be that late? He looked at the darkened window, half-expecting to see the first light of dawn in the sky, but it hadn't happened yet. He stopped what he was doing, left his room, went inside the kitchen where he drank a glass of water—cold, tasting of moss. Through the kitchen doorway he could see Mike sitting in the living room, staring blankly at a test card on the TV. It was strange, soundless, just this spooky series of rainbow colors. Mike had been still and silent ever since they'd come back from the precinct house, and the depth of his quiet emphasized the emptiness of the apartment, the fact that *she* wasn't there any more, that *she* would never be coming back. . . .

Never was an odd word, Peter thought. When he'd come home he'd taken out an old scrapbook of pictures, looking at snapshots of his mother and father, his *real* father, thinking how dated their clothes were, how their smiles in all that sunlight seemed doomed, destined to death, and it struck him that never again, never in the history of the world, would his parents be together again. Unless there was something after death, a thought he balked at because in his heart he was a scientist, he understood the disciplines of science, the quantifications and the formulae and the experiments that sometimes gave you results. What experiment could ever prove there was something beyond the grave? There wasn't one. If there was anything out there, it was shrouded and silent and locked in a dark privacy. When he'd closed the book, he'd gone inside the bathroom and shut the door and cried, realizing the uselessness of tears, the waste of energy involved, and time passing, time he could put to more practical use.

Now he looked at his stepfather for a moment, wanting to cross the floor, touch him, maybe put his arms around the man, as if that might ease their sense of loss.

He said, "Can I get you something? A glass of water maybe?"

Mike turned his head slowly. The test card flickered. When he spoke his voice was hoarse. "Nothing. But thanks."

"I thought . . ." Peter faltered, not knowing what he meant to say.

Mike was staring at him.

"Thanks anyhow," he said again.

Peter went back to his room and closed the door. Christ, it was hard not to feel sorry for Mike. He sat down at his worktable, staring at the assorted devices lying in front of him. Maybe it was a harebrained idea, this gadget; maybe it was going to prove nothing in the end but a waste of time. Sometimes an idea for a project came into his mind out of nowhere, like some magic thing conjured up out of the unconscious; at other times a project was imposed upon him by classroom demands. But this was the first time he'd ever felt such an urgent necessity to do something, even if as he worked at it he had recurring feelings that it wasn't going to do any good. He couldn't afford to believe that. He couldn't afford to be pessimistic.

He owed that much to her.

Then he felt he wanted to cry again, but he held the feeling back. She wouldn't have wanted that. He stared at the closed door; she'd never appear there again, scolding him for not getting enough sleep. Never . . . damn, he wasn't going to think in terms of never; he wanted to pass through that stage. He concentrated on the objects on the table once more, picking up the camera, a Yashica, and the eyepiece of the telescope, testing the screw he had made to bolt the camera to the scope. He was pretty certain it would hold without loosening, provided it didn't get accidentally knocked. But that was another chance he'd have to take. You couldn't get round the possibility of an accident.

Suddenly restless, he got up from the table and walked round the room. She'd always joked about his room,

about the mess, the chaos, but the fact was, he knew
where to find anything. It might have looked haphazard
to an outsider, but he'd arranged everything exactly
where he wanted it. When he needed something—a text-
book, a tool, anything—he could find it in a second. He
stood at the window and looked out across the darkness
for a time, wondering about his mother's killer, wondering about the kind of mind that would produce an act like
that. A deranged mind, obviously. The kind of personality that might seek help from a shrink. A shrink like
Elliott. *I'm not protecting anybody.* Elliott had said that.
What was there about the shrink he didn't like? A certain
aloofness, maybe. A coldness? He wasn't sure. He just
couldn't imagine his mother going there as often as she
had; he couldn't even imagine what had made his mother
go there anyhow, unless it was connnected with the death
of his father. . . .

He felt sad again, a biting sadness that seemed to claw
at some place in his chest. You don't need this, he told
himself. You need to act, you need to find out if Elliott is
really protecting a patient. So you use the only tools you
know how to use: the tools of science, of technology. He
picked up the camera, held it to the window, looked
through the lens. It worked beautifully; he could see a
perfect enlargement of the window on the other side of
the street, down to the sight of an illuminated fishtank
behind open drapes, he could see the flickering shapes of
red swordtails as they moved between swaying plants. He
felt pleased with the thing. All that was left now was to
attach the electric motor. When he'd done that and enclosed the whole thing in the steel box, he'd be ready.

He sat down at the table and calculated quickly: assume the average length of an appointment with a psychiatrist is one hour, assume his office hours begin at nine
thirty or at ten. Therefore, if you set the time-lapse dial of
the electric motor to operate the shutter at fifteen minute
intervals, beginning at nine thirty, you have a reasonably
good chance of getting the kind of photographs you want.
If the first appointment is at nine thirty, you get a picture
of that person arriving. If it isn't until ten, you still get a
picture.

He set the whole thing back down on the worktable,

attached the small motor to the camera by means of a
strong metal clasp and a wire that ran from the motor to
the shutter release with an extra attachment affixed to the
film advancer. Then he tested it: it worked perfectly. He
loaded the film, put the gadget inside the metal box,
padlocked the box. Finished, he was exhausted, and with
the fatigue came a sense of despair, of how farfetched his
plan really might turn out to be. All kinds of things could
go wrong: there might be an accident or Elliott might
take the day off or his office hours might be different from
those Peter had supposed or his patients might be late or
early for their appointments.

A long shot. A long, long shot.

But what else could he do? What else could he do with
this burning sense he had for revenge?

He threw some papers off his bed and lay down. He
knew he wouldn't sleep. He closed his eyes, but the images
he had scared him, sickened him—that razor falling time
and again into his mother's skin, her blood flowing out,
draining out of her.

He listened once more to the conversation between
Marino and Elliott, playing it through his head as if it
were tape recorded. And then he thought once again of
his mother; this fucking terrible sadness—how could he
fight that with science or technology? They were goddamn
useless when it came to emotion. They didn't help.

He had a tight feeling in his throat.

He sat upright on the edge of the bed with his eyes
closed because he didn't want to cry again; he wanted to
squeeze the tears away. In frustration, he banged his
hands together and he thought: I loved you. I loved you
deeply.

And now you're gone.

6

Marino groaned. He must have fallen briefly asleep after
calling his wife to say he wouldn't be home—a call she'd
heard too many times, a message she knew by heart—but
now he snapped his eyes open as the telephone on his
desk rang. Sleepily he reached out to pick it up; at the
same time he noticed the tickets to the ball game that were

tucked in at the edge of his blotter, something he'd promised his kids. The kids, he thought; he was dragging them up in a world of broken promises.

"Lieutenant. This is Betty Luce."

"Yeah," Marino said.

"I'm outside the apartment," the woman said.

"And?" Marino heard himself sound grumpy. Waking, when he hadn't had any sleep, was one of his less pleasant experiences; now he felt drained.

"It's all quiet."

"Good," Marino said.

"I didn't see her come out. She's still in there."

Marino reached for the tickets to the game. "Did you take a break?"

"A couple of hours ago," the woman said. "It was only for coffee. . . ."

Human, all too human, Marino thought. Sometimes he wished cops could be replaced by automatons, things that didn't have to grab a cup of coffee or a sandwich or drift off into the world of sleep.

"The apartment lights were on when I left. They just went out about five minutes ago," the woman said. "Also, I called and hung up when she answered, just to be sure."

"Fine," Marino said. "I'll see you get relieved as soon as I can."

"Okay, Lieutenant."

Marino put the telephone down, rubbed his eyes, and then walked up and down his office just to stay awake. It had been a long night, and a longer day lay ahead.

7

She took off the padded bra.

She dropped it to the floor.

She undid the zipper of her skirt, let it fall around her, stepped out of it.

She removed the silk panties, kicking them free of her feet.

Naked, she stood in the middle of the room.

She stared at the telephone. It depressed her.

It depressed her because it made her think of Elliott.

She didn't want that.

She scooped up the clothes and put them in a closet.

There was a pain between her legs.

She reached down and touched herself.

A flock of memories crowded her like ravenous black birds. It was as if the sky were darkened, the sun eclipsed one final time.

Why didn't you catch the ball?

Don't you like the game? Too rough for you?

She wasn't sure what to say. Her tongue felt heavy and swollen inside her mouth. Somewhere it was autumn, there was a playing field, there were kids screaming as they chased something, rooks flew upwards out of the stark trees and headed straight for the bronze sun as if they sought disaster in the sky.

Too rough for you, eh?

She saw their faces stare at her. Their naked little faces in the changing room. Water was running somewhere. Somebody was whistling. Something splashed. She wished they wouldn't stare like that. She hadn't done anything wrong.

She took her hand away from between her legs.

Now there was another voice: a woman's this time, sounding imperative and sonorous, the kind of voice accustomed to issuing orders and having them obeyed. Her mother. You understand, dear, there are certain things you do not do . . . certain things that are simply not done.

I haven't done anything wrong.

Your sister tells me she found you . . .

Found me what?

Playing, shall we say, in a certain fashion.

It's not true—

I'm afraid it is true.

My sister's a liar—

I don't think so, dear—

She is! She is! She's a liar!

Oh, hardly . . .

She went inside the bathroom.

She looked at herself in the mirror.

She remembered now the strangely luscious feel of taffeta, the thick layers of material lying against her skin, the strange out-of-the-body feeling she'd experienced then, and with it the certain knowledge that she was hideously trapped, imprisoned, contained by the contours of her own flesh.

Mirror, mirror.

Answer me.

Deadening silence.

A twinge of pain.

She went close to the mirror; close enough to see the flaws in her skin through the makeup, close enough to see the pores, the cracks, the lines of time. Then she drew away from the image. She shut her eyes.

All you had to do, Elliott, was to give your permission.

A small thing. Your signature. Your okay.

The operation.

But you didn't. You didn't because you don't know the hellish nature of this kind of trap. You just don't understand. . . .

I'll kill again, she thought. And you'll know it was me again.

She felt tears run down her face, tracking thinly over the makeup, bitter rivulets she couldn't stop, couldn't hold back. She caught the memory, months old, of another blade, of raising that same blade in her hands, bringing it down, bringing it down between her legs—

She went out of the bathroom and picked up the telephone.

Without dialling a number she said, "Help me, Levy. You *must* help me!"

She put the receiver down.

She drew her hand away from it, watched the hand rise in the air, felt it fall, felt it stop between her legs, felt it touch the thin layer of gauze that was wrapped around the shaft of the penis.

As if scalded, she pulled her hand away. It was a nightmare too old, too familiar, a nightmare whose end she couldn't see.

FIVE

1

It was that time of morning when the city felt clean in its emptiness, when the lack of traffic on the streets, the absence of people, suggested that maybe some silent nuclear attack had taken place during the hours of darkness. A neutron bomb, Peter thought, the kind that kills all the inhabitants but leaves the buildings standing. He rode his bicycle almost carelessly, cruising through DON'T WALK signs, cutting past stop lights, feeling some extraordinary exhilaration at being alone in the streets. Even the buildings seemed not to reach upwards like they usually did; rather, they appeared dwarfed in the clarity of dawn. He pedalled hard, cycling past the empty storefronts and luncheonettes that hadn't yet opened. There was even a slight breeze, clean and crystal in a way that surprised him.

When he reached the street where Elliott's office was located, he slowed his bike a little, took Elliott's card from his pocket, checked the address again, and then began to look for the number. When he found it he paused, stared at the wooden door and the brass plaque with the psychiatrist's name; then he wheeled diagonally across the street to a NO PARKING sign. He took a padlock from his jacket and bolted the bike to the sign. As he worked, he glanced once more across at the door of Elliott's office—nothing, no sign of life—and he couldn't help thinking of his mother coming out of there yesterday, even if yesterday seemed to him now an illogical number of years ago. Subjective time, he thought, something measured by some inner psychological clock.

He opened the metal box fastened to the rack of the bike, turning the key in the padlock. He reached inside and touched the camera, made sure that the telescope was mounted securely, that the small electric motor was functioning properly. He switched on the motor, heard it whir quietly, then he checked that the lens of the camera was properly positioned against a small aperture cut into the metal box. What if it doesn't work? he wondered. Imponderables: somebody could come along and hacksaw the whole padlock off and that would be the end of that plan, or maybe the photographs would be timed badly, missing the people who entered and left Elliott's office, in which case he'd have a set of terrific shots of a closed door. You had to take a chance, he told himself. He closed the hinged lid of the metal box, making sure once again that everything was in working order, then he locked the box and rattled both padlocks with his fingers. They were secure; everything was as secure as he could make it.

He walked a few paces away, turned, then stared back across the street at the door of the psychiatrist's office. Still no sign of life. Only the first glimmer of morning sunlight, burning against the brass nameplate, suggested movement.

He rubbed his hands, realizing suddenly that there was a chill in the morning air, a factor he'd been too preoccupied to notice before. Later he'd come back for the bike and the camera and see what he might have captured.

2

Elliott woke in his office, his body stiff from the angle he'd been sleeping in. He groaned quietly, rose from the sofa, and went inside the bathroom where he splashed his face and neck with cold water. Drying himself off, he walked to the desk and looked at his wristwatch. 8:05. It wasn't his custom to sleep this late; it must have been on account of the Equanil he'd taken the night before, which might also have explained the slight nausea he felt as he drew the drapes back from the window. The morning light was stunning; blinking, he stepped away. He took his shirt from the back of the chair where he'd left it last night, put it on, then pulled on his pants. He checked the answering machine on his desk but there were no messages—nothing, nothing from Bobbi. He fastened his cuff links and sat behind the desk and gazed at the telephone, wondering why she hadn't called. Sooner or later, he thought, the telephone will ring and she'll be on the other end of the line. . . . But he didn't want to think about her now. He flipped open the pages of his appointments book and just as he was doing so he heard his front doorbell ring. The mailman, he thought, a package, a registered letter. He went out through the reception room to the lobby and drew the chain on the front door.

But it wasn't the mailman.

It was Anne.

Elliott, surprised, didn't move for a time.

"Do I get asked in, dear?" Anne said.

"Of course, I . . ."

"Surprised to see me, I imagine," she said.

He held the door wide. She brushed past him, her hands in the pockets of her tweed jacket. He noticed the leather patches stitched to the elbows, the baggy flannel pants, the brown shoes of a kind that might once have been called sensible. She left in her passage a faint scent of alcohol, gin maybe; he wasn't sure. He followed her inside the reception room, then through to his office, and what struck him, rather forcefully, was how incongruous it felt to have his wife here, as if this were his domain alone; a secret aspect of his life that had nothing to do with her. With the feeling came a slight sense of resentment.

"I came down on an early train," she said, looking around the office, going to the desk, picking up the framed photograph of herself that sat there. She stared at it, then set it down as if it disgusted her. She swung around to face him. "You look as if you didn't get much of a night's sleep, my dear. . . ."

"Is that supposed to mean something?" he asked. He sighed, thinking: I don't need to start my day like this, I don't need a scene with Anne.

Anne shook her head. She wandered around the room, looking at the shelf of books, touching the handles of locked cabinets. He sensed something dangerous all at once, something destructive. He could imagine her pulling the books down, breaking the locks on the cabinets, smashing things.

"The early train is rather nice," she said. "They serve drinks. I availed myself of that service, of course."

"Of course," Elliott said.

She leaned against the desk, staring at the sofa. "Is that where your so-called patients lie down? Do they lie there and divulge their miserable little secrets to you? Do they *trust you*, my dear?" She smiled in a thin way.

"Sometimes," he said. He picked up his necktie and draped it beneath his collar, nervously making a knot. "Why did you come here, Anne?"

"I couldn't sleep," she said. "I found myself at what you might conveniently call a loose end. I thought, well . . . I might as well take a quick trip into town and see how my husband is doing. The mountain goes to Mohammed, so to speak."

He watched her wander back to the books again. She reached up, took one down, flicked through the pages. She laughed, for no reason he could understand, although there was a vaguely hysterical edge to the sound.

"Do you actually read all this stuff?" she said.

"I try to keep up," he said.

"I try to keep up," she said, mimicking him. *"The Treatment of Schizophrenic Psychosis by Direct Analytic Therapy.* What the hell is that supposed to mean?"

Elliott folded his arms, said nothing. He knew this mood too well, the bitterness, the underlying savagery.

She replaced the book and looked along the other titles.

"Nothing on how to fix a marriage, dear? Nothing like a self-help marital manual?"

He still didn't speak.

"Fuck you," she said. "You leave me in that ghastly house, you never even bother . . ." She paused, close to tears, her lower lip trembling in a way he found distasteful. Anne, he thought. And for a moment he wanted to reach out and touch her in some way, to silence the sound of a marriage falling apart, the brutal noise of the heart's assassination. But it had gone past that a long time ago, and now there was nothing he could do.

"Today is the day," she said.

"What day do you mean, Anne?"

"Shall I lie on the couch and let you analyze me?"

"What day are you talking about, Anne?"

She put the palm of her hand flat against her forehead. "I have made an appointment to see Burbage—"

"Burbage? Why?"

"He *is* the family lawyer, after all."

Elliott shook his head. "I don't have to ask, do I?"

"No dear, asking would be utterly superfluous in the circumstances—the answer is obvious."

"I don't even have to ask you to reconsider, do I?"

She laughed again. "If we're honest, perfectly and splendidly honest with each other, we would realize that our marriage is dead tissue. . . . A skin graft is quite out of the question."

For a moment he didn't know quite what he felt. Maybe there was an iota of relief somewhere inside, but there was also an awareness of failure, disappointment; he hadn't been able to make the marriage work.

"Papers will be served at the appropriate time," she said. She looked at him coldly. "If grounds were needed, I have grounds in bounteous supply."

He stared down at the floor, touching the fringe of a rug with his foot.

"Do you realize the last time we had . . ." She paused, laughing again. "Do you realize the last time we had conjugal relations, my love?"

"I haven't kept a calendar," he answered.

"Ah. Inside my head there's this tiny abacus, and I do keep track. . . . We are talking about a period of almost nine months, dear. By any standards, it's a long time. By the most chaste of standards, it's preposterous. You leave me without alternatives, darling."

Darling. How cold she could make the word sound. He watched her face which, in the morning light, was pale and swollen, excess flesh hanging from the cheeks, purple pouches beneath the eyes.

"Whatever," she said. "I thought I'd stop by and tell you my decision, so that the papers, when they *are* served, will not cause you undue trauma."

She picked up the photograph of herself again and, with a sudden violent flick of her wrist, smashed it against the side of the desk so that sparks of glass, shattering and spraying the air, fell to the rug.

"I don't imagine you'll be needing it, not now," she said.

He stared at the flecks of glass, gleaming in the light as if they were stones once thought to be precious but found, under a jeweler's eyepiece, to be quite worthless.

Anne walked to the door.

There, she turned around, raised her hand in a limp wave, and said, "I can find my own way out. Don't trouble yourself."

He watched the door close. After a moment, he went down on his hands and knees and began to pick up the shards of glass.

As he was doing so his telephone rang. The sound startled him, causing him to move his hand sharply so that a tiny splinter of glass entered the tip of a finger, embedding itself just beneath the skin. With his other hand he picked up the receiver, half-expecting it to be Bobbi, half-expecting to hear that strange wild voice, but it wasn't.

"Dr. Elliott?"

He recognized the voice as that of a female patient, a certain Evelyn Hunt who lived permanently at the Waldorf Towers and whose main problem in life seemed to concern her relationship with her immense wealth and the guilt involved. She collected photographs of atrocities cut from newspapers and magazines, most of them depicting Cambodian or Vietnamese refugees or corpses napalmed in the hinterlands of Abyssinia. Lately, she'd become concerned about events in Angola.

"I wonder if you might squeeze me in today at some point," she was saying.

"I can try," Elliott said. He opened his appointments book. "I have thirty minutes between eleven-fifteen and eleven forty-five, Mrs. Hunt."

The woman was quiet a moment. "Frankly," she said. "I'm rather upset. My dog, Patrick, died in the night."

"Oh dear—"

"And only this morning I received word in the mail that the child I was sponsoring in Brazil—Roseanna, you remember?—is suffering from malaria."

Elliott sucked at the sliver of glass in his fingertip.

"I'm sure we can put these things in some perspective," he said, trying to sound cheerful, trying not to think of Anne's visit. He reached for a pen and made a note to write a prescription for Tranxene, the glue of Evelyn Hunt's life.

"Thank you, Dr. Elliott," the woman said.

"No problem, I assure you. See you at eleven-fifteen, Mrs. Hunt."

Elliott put the receiver down.

For a time he didn't move, thinking again of Anne. Maybe she was right, maybe it *was* for the best; you shouldn't waste energy trying to resuscitate a corpse. He closed his eyes. What it came down to was the fact that he had more pressing matters on his mind.

Still, there was a certain lingering sadness lying like some bloated raincloud at the back of his mind. He sighed, opened his eyes, searched for the piece of paper on which he'd written the address and telephone number of Bobbi's Dr. Levy. He looked at his watch, realized it was still too early to call the number, then folded the paper neatly and placed it under an onyx paperweight—a gift, he remembered, from Anne, a gift belonging to that time when the pretences of marriage masked the hollowness of content.

3

Norma had already gone when Liz woke: She felt puffy from sleep, from the effects of the sleeping pill, her limbs heavy, her mind sluggish. There was a note on the kitchen table, written in Norma's copperplate handwriting. It read:

Your couch is uncomfortable & I slept real bad but no bogeyladies came anyways. A man from Cleveland is expecting you at seven thirty on the dot at room 234 of the Parkway Hotel. Your friendly escort person, Norma.

Shit, Liz thought, wishing she could crumple the paper and stuff it into the garbage disposal. Seven thirty. How could she get herself into the right frame of mind by that time, for Christ's sake? She set the note up against a milk carton and gazed at it, wondering if she could call Norma for a reprieve. . . . What the hell, do you or don't you need the money? Moving in a somnambulistic manner, she went to the telephone and dialled Max's number. The secretary put her through almost at once.

"I was expecting you to call," Max said.

"Would you believe I was involved in other things?" Liz said.

"Where you're concerned, I'd believe anything," Max said. There was a click and Max asked, "Can you hold? I got somebody on the other line."

"Oh, fuck, Max—why do I have to hold? I mean, I'm first in line, right?"

Max made a hollow sighing sound. "Yeah. Okay. Listen, you were supposed to bring me approximately a grand, honey."

"Like I said, I was detained, Max. Since when did I ever let you down about delivering cash?"

"True—there's always a first time."

"Not with me, sweetheart."

"Well, your AutoTron rose to fifteen sixty eight. So whoever the horse is you're listening to, he must have to be feeding from the correct bag, kid."

Liz opened a drawer and found her small calculator. She tapped the keys a moment. "Can you get me some more, Max?"

"*More?*"

"Yeah, more."

Rustle of paper, a telephone ringing, Max sighing again. "How much this time?"

"Another five yards," Liz said.

"You want to be careful of that street talk, you know? I assume five yards means five hundred?"

"Yeah." Liz switched her calculator off. "Listen, I'll get the bread to you today."

"Before closing."

"Before closing," she said.

"Bubbles have this habit of bursting, Liz."

"Yeah, but I got a feeling this one is going to float some ways longer. Talk at you later."

"Hold on. What happened to you anyhow? I expected you before this."

"If I told you, Maxie dear, you wouldn't believe me anyhow."

"Listen, I'm gung ho on fairy tales, hard luck stories, and fables in general—"

"What I could tell you wouldn't fit any of those categories."

"If you say so."

"Later, Max." And she hung up.

A man from Cleveland at seven thirty. That would just about cover the money she'd need for Max. She thought for a moment, wondering if and when her run of market luck would collapse, then she dialled her bank. She gave her account number and name and asked for her balance. She had more than seven thousand in her checking account and slightly less than fifteen and a half in her savings; she also had ten thousand stashed away in a certificate of deposit at an annual interest rate of 11.7%. She picked up her calculator and tapped at the keys again. Barring accidents—like Marino arresting her for homicide—she could quit the game with about $60,000 in realizable assets, which was sufficient for whatever purpose she would decide upon later.

She brewed some coffee, checked the time—it was just after midday—and then she sat at the kitchen table, sipping the coffee, smoking a cigarette. Then there was the sound, so abrupt that it startled her, of a knock on the door. She tightened the cord of her robe and went to the front door and put her eye to the peephole. When she saw who it was she opened the door. Marino, wearing a lightweight raincoat, stepped inside.

"Talk of the devil," she said.

"Meaning me?"

"Meaning you, right. I was just thinking about you—"

"Nasty thoughts, I hope."

"They weren't the most kind, Lieutenant." She walked towards the kitchen, the cop following her.

"I smell fresh coffee," Marino said.

"Help yourself." Liz sat down at the table, stubbed her

cigarette, while Marino poured some coffee and then leaned against the refrigerator door, watching her.

"You must be in a pretty nice racket, Liz," he said.

She glanced at him.

He said, "I mean the rent on this place alone . . ." He whistled. He ran a hand, in a weary way, across his jaw.

"I work hard," Liz said.

"Top dollar, huh?"

Liz lit another cigarette. She wished she didn't let this cop get to her the way he did. "Is there some reason for this visit? Social call maybe? Or have you brought your handcuffs?"

The cop smiled. He touched his moustache, as though it were an irritant. "I told you I'd be keeping tabs, didn't I?"

"Yeah. You don't want to lose your prime suspect, do you?"

Marino sipped his coffee and made a face, then he sat down at the other end of the table and yawned. "You're still pretty damn high on my list, lady."

"And all you need is a motive, right?"

"A motive I could dream up in my sleep," the cop said. "This coffee tastes like crude oil."

"Pardon me. I'll brew some to your liking, sir, if you have the time."

"Sarcasm I don't need." Marino put his cup down.

"How many times, for God's sake, do I need to tell you I didn't kill the woman? You want it in blood?"

"Hey," Marino said. "I came here in friendship. And what do I get? Abuse. Sarcasm. A policeman's lot is not a happy one, they say."

"Friendship?" Liz asked. "Your kind of friendship I don't go out of my way for. It would make it a helluva lot easier if you'd believe me, you know that?"

The cop smiled and reached for something on the table. *Norma's note.* Liz put out her hand to grab it away, but Marino had a firm grip on it and was leaning back in his chair, reading it, shaking his head.

"I could interpret this as being highly unlawful, Liz."

Liz said nothing.

"Seven thirty at the Parkway Hotel. A gentleman from

Cleveland. I assume you're not going there for a game of poker. . . ."

"That happens to be private correspondence, Lieutenant."

Marino put the piece of paper down against the milk carton. He was still shaking his head. "It has—how would you say?—a dubious ring to it?"

"Call it what you like. If you want to go on talking to me, Lieutenant, I think I'd like my lawyer present."

Marino smiled. "Lawyer? I told you, this is a social call."

"By your definition—"

"Only doing my duty, Liz. Making sure you're still around. Some people have this weird habit of skipping town when they've been asked *specifically* to remain available, you know that? It's highly unreasonable, but some folks just vanish." He paused, stuck his hands in the pockets of his coat, and added, "Anyhow, like I said, you're still numero uno on my little black list. And unless something positive turns up to the contrary, kid, I might even have to book you."

Liz watched him. What the fuck kind of game was he playing anyhow? She had the unsettling feeling that his bluff was something you just didn't call, and she wanted more than anything else to say, *So book me and get it over with.* She sipped her coffee and remained silent. Marino drummed his fingers on the table for a moment. Then he said, "I've got to tell you, Liz. If something doesn't break real soon, I'll have to make a decision concerning your future, which right at this moment doesn't exactly look too bright. It would be a pity. I like you, in a funny kinda way."

It crossed her mind that he might be looking for a freebie, but she dismissed that. He had "family man" stamped all over him, like it was a suit of armor he wore. She watched him yawn again. Then he said, "Anyhow, glad to see you haven't skipped. Keep your nose clean."

"I will."

"You better," he said, rising. He went to the door where he turned around and smiled. "You either use too much coffee or you're buying a real cheap brand. Try some French Roast next time. Or espresso. You'll get great results."

"Thanks for the hint."

"Just one of Marino's Many Household Tips, Liz. Be good. And beware."

She didn't move. She heard the outer door close.

Beware.

What the hell was that supposed to mean?

She listened to the hollow silence of the apartment for a time, wishing the telephone would ring or the refrigerator motor kick on or a faucet suddenly start to drip— anything to whip the profound quiet that had settled like a web throughout the rooms. She got up and went to the window and looked out. She saw Marino, diminutive from this height, cross the street and get inside a parked car. The car pulled away from the sidewalk.

In another car, parked some distance away from the one Marino had just entered, a blonde woman sat with her head tilted back against the seat. She watched the street, yawning now and again, covering her mouth with her hands. Once, she glanced at the apartment building entrance; then she looked at herself in the mirror, tilting it towards her for a good view, noticing how glazed her eyes were and how dark the circles under the lower lashes.

4

The patient was a young man who had recently attempted to kill himself; he had done so by slashing his underarms with a butcher's knife—an attempt, Elliott realized, that was some form of revenge against his mother. In strictly Freudian terms, it was classically simple. He had been coming to Elliott now for several weeks, each session producing more and more vehement statements about his mother. Elliott, sitting back in his chair with the tips of his fingers pressed together beneath his chin, had developed the habit of hearing only key phrases, which was what he did now, occasionally nodding his head, making a small gesture, or leaning forward to touch the onyx paperweight. He had moments sometimes when he wanted to say: *You think you have problems; would you like to hear some of mine?* But he understood that unless he were perceived as being somehow infallible, his worth to his patients was drastically diminished. Now, half-closing his eyes, he heard the young man's drone. "Wanted a daughter, not a son . . ." My wife just told me she's divorcing me, Elliott thought. Would you care to hear that? Elliott nodded. "One time, I remember, she put a ribbon in my hair. . . . You got to understand, like, I was about six at the time, yeah, six, maybe seven, and she'd let my hair grow in these long fucking curls. I didn't know if I was a girl or a boy or what. . . ." Elliott smiled sympathetically. "The big trauma was like when I went off to school. . . . I mean, you can dig what they called me there, huh?" Divorce, Elliott thought. How empty the word sounded. How dreadfully final. He stared at the young man, who was straightening out a paper clip, twisting it this way and that, then trying to roll it flat between his palms. Finally, he gave up and dropped the twisted metal in an ashtray. *"They said I was a goddamn sissy, couldn't do this right, couldn't do that, and because of this fucking woman who wouldn't let me be what I wanted to be, which was male, which was the goddamn sex I was born with. . . ."*

"When did your father die?" Elliott asked.

"Before I was born," the young man said. He was sweating heavily his forehead glistening.

"What did your mother tell you about your father?"

"You want it verbatim?"

Elliott nodded.

"She said he was a prick. Couldn't keep from screwing anything that moved. Said she had to make sure I didn't grow up like him."

"But you feel certain about your sex now, don't you?" Elliott asked.

The young man shrugged. "Sometimes, I don't know. I get this horrible thought, though. I'm not going to feel right until *she's* dead."

"Do you want to kill her?"

"It's crossed my mind. But I wouldn't."

Elliott leaned forward. "In trying to kill yourself,

would you say you were *really* trying to kill your mother?"

"Uh—it's possible."

"You didn't really want to destroy *yourself*, did
you?"

The young man looked blank..

Elliott said, "You wanted to kill her. In the emotional
sense anyhow. If you'd succeeded, she'd have been filled
with remorse, am I right?" He thought of Anne, wondered if Anne had such a suicidal tendency, wondered if
she were capable of killing herself so that he would feel
like the murderer.

"Yeah, maybe. I wanted to hurt her, real bad."

Elliott was silent. He stared past the young man at the
framed pictures on the walls. In the direct sunlight of the
early afternoon one could only see the glass shining, not
the prints beneath.

"Do you still want to hurt her?" Elliott asked.

"I don't know," the young man said.

"Do you think I should talk with her?"

"I don't think *she'd* talk with *you*—" The young man,
brushing a curl from his forehead, smiled. It was a bleak
smile. "She thinks head-doctors are poison."

"Poison," Elliott said, and laughed. "We get called all
kinds of names." He paused, picked up his letter opener.
"You're not living at home now, are you?"

"I rented a room. It's not much."

"Does she know where to find you?"

"She'll find out. She always finds out."

Elliott heard his telephone.

"Excuse me," he said to the young man as he picked
up the receiver.

The voice on the other end of the line said, "Dr.
Elliott? This is George Levy. I understand you left a
message about wanting to see me."

"That's right," Elliott said.

"Can you give me some idea of what you want?"

Elliott paused. Then he said, "It concerns a patient of
mine. A former patient, I should say. It's imperative that
I see you as soon as I can. I'm in a consultation at the
moment—can I call you back?"

"I'm a little mystified," Levy said. "Why the urgency?"

"I'd prefer to talk to you in person, Dr. Levy."

There was a silence; Elliott could hear the other man flick the pages of a book.

"I don't know when it would be convenient," Levy said after a while. "Why don't you ring me when you're free?"

"Thanks. I'll do that."

Elliott put the receiver down. He looked at his young patient, then glanced at his watch.

"We're just about out of time, I'm afraid."

The young man nodded. "Same time next week?"

"Certainly." Elliott got up. He thought: I could talk to Anne, ask her to think things over, see if it can be made good again. Had it ever been any good? He walked out into the reception room with the young man.

"I'll see you next week, Arthur. If anything comes up in the meantime, you can always reach me."

The young man smiled, then he was gone.

Elliott looked round the empty waiting room, then returned to his office where—after hesitating, after wondering how he was going to approach the subject of Bobbi with another psychiatrist—he picked up his telephone and dialled Levy's number.

Even before it was answered in Levy's office, he put the receiver down. Think, he told himself. Think it through carefully before you talk with Levy. The problem was still the same: the idea that you were protecting a killer. He rubbed his jaw and looked at the telephone, wishing that Bobbi would ring back. Wishing he could just talk with her, locate her, then he'd know what to do for sure.

But she hadn't called and he had no idea where she was now.

He dialled Levy's number.

5

It was one of those old-fashioned stores that pretend to cater to a diminishing species—the gentleman. There were racks of tweed sportscoats, shelves of toilet requisites, expensive imported lotions and after-shaves, handcrafted leather boots and equestrian accoutrements, saddles and riding crops and jodhpurs; there were shotguns, pith helmets, assorted decoy ducks, a multitude of fishing poles and brightly-colored flies. More than anything else, it suggested the paraphernalia of an empire that the United States had never possessed in the first place. The clerks were hushed and reverential, moving around in a manner that indicated they were gliding on smooth rollers. Here was a counterfeit history, a sense of antiquity stolen from another culture, and everybody spoke, it seemed, with English accents.

She felt out of place; a discordant element.

When the clerk approached her in his dark jacket and pinstripe pants she wanted to back out of the store, make an excuse, claim she'd come to the wrong place. But she didn't. When she explained what she wanted—"a gift for an old friend, of course"—the clerk simply nodded and disappeared behind a counter, returning a moment later with a tray of objects, which he held in front of her as if he were a waiter in a gourmet restaurant tempting a customer with a lavish assortment of desserts.

She stared at the array of objects. The clerk, waiting, said nothing. Finally, she chose one with a pearl handle. The clerk said it was an excellent choice and made some comment lamenting the passing of such instruments. "We live, madam, in a disposable society," he remarked. "I trust the day will not come when we eventually dispose of ourselves."

She smiled. She watched him place the pearl-handled thing inside a leather case. She saw him drop it inside a bag discreetly embossed with the name of the store. She paid, imagining for a moment that the sight of cash distressed the clerk. But he apparently recovered. "I'm sure your friend will find that to his liking," he said.

She stepped outside into the sunlight of the afternoon, dropping the paper bag inside her purse. She took out her black glasses and put them on because the sudden harshness of the sun had made her blink.

It was close to five when Peter went to get his bicycle from its place opposite Elliott's office. He was relieved to find nobody had tampered with it. He looked inside the metal box, made sure everything was in its place, then unlocked the padlock that bound the bike to the NO PARKING sign. He pedalled quickly away; he could hardly wait to have the photographs printed.

She watched the entranceway.

Nothing much happened.

A florist's delivery man went inside with a bouquet of flowers.

A brown van from United Parcels drew up, then pulled away without making a delivery.

A beat cop strolled past, then disappeared round the corner.

She looked up at the windows of the building. They were flattened, like beaten gold, by the failing sun.

Sooner or later the woman would come out. Sooner or later she would have to.

Peter parked his bicycle in the parking lot behind an apartment building, padlocking it to the bars provided for bikes. He removed the metal box from the rack and went inside the building. He couldn't wait for the elevator, so he rushed the stairs to the third floor, then he searched the doors for number three five four. When he found it he pressed the doorbell, waited, and then the door was opened by a small dark-haired woman in her early fifties.

"Is Gunther home?" Peter asked, clutching the box hard to his side.

The woman said something in German, then turned her face along the corridor and called out Gunther's name. After a moment, Peter could make out the shape of his friend at the end of the dark lobby of the apartment—unmistakable, with that strange Afro he wore and the way he stooped to detract from his height.

"Didn't think you were coming," Gunther said. "Wanna come in?"

Peter stepped inside, the woman closed the door, muttered something else in German, and then Peter followed Gunther into a side room.

"You said you'd pay," Gunther said. "I wouldn't ask,

you being a friend, but I'm pretty short of bread right now."

"I brought the bucks," Peter said. He took two crumpled five dollar bills from his jacket and handed them to Gunther. The other kid stared at them, as if he suspected counterfeits. Then, seemingly satisfied, he stuffed them in his jeans.

"Here's the film," Peter said.

Gunther took the roll. "I don't see the urgency, man."

"Just develop the film, okay?"

Gunther shrugged. He closed the door of what was obviously his bedroom—a messy room, whose walls were covered with posters of an hallucinogenic nature; mushrooms and patterns created out of surrealistic marijuana leaves and circles of smoke. Then he opened the door of a large closet, which Peter saw was his darkroom.

"I prefer to work alone," Gunther said. "But if you keep quiet and don't get in my way, you can come inside. Okay?"

"You won't hear anything from me," Peter said.

They went inside the darkroom. Gunther turned on the red light. Peter surveyed the rows of trays, the bottles of chemicals. He watched as Gunther opened the film and bent over the trays. The red light cast a weird glow over everything. Gunther put the film into a developing tank, then worked at something Peter couldn't see because the kid had his back to him.

"How long does this take?" Peter asked.

"You said you'd be quiet, man," Gunther answered.

"Okay, okay. I'm a little impatient, that's all."

"A *little?*"

Peter stared at the shelves on the walls. There were bottles fixed with abbreviated words like DEV and FIX and STOP. For a moment he wished he were interested enough to have a darkroom of his own, but it was too late to worry about that now. Around him there were wires from which clothespins hung suspended. Peter whistled quietly through his teeth, then Gunther looked at him in a chilly way. So he was quiet. It all seemed to be taking such a goddamn long time. He tried to relax.

After a while, Gunther said, "What kinda pictures are these, man?"

"What do you mean?"

Gunther hung a few up by the pins. "They're like the door of a house or something."

Peter stared at the first few shots. He felt a terrible sense of disappointment. They showed only the door of Elliott's office. Gunther produced another one.

"This one's got somebody in it, at least."

Peter looked at it. It was a photograph of a young man coming out of the office. After that there was another sequence of uninteresting ones.

Three of the door.

One that showed a mailman moving out of shot.

Then a lady with a dog.

Then, tantalizingly, one of the door half open—but with no figure visible.

There were a couple of blurred shots of people just passing.

"Hey, these are great," Gunther said. "You could really make yourself a name, man. Some new kind of avant-garde photography. Pictures that don't mean anything, you know?"

"Just keep developing," Peter said.

Gunther shrugged and went back to work.

Two of the door.

A drunk, apparently, swaying past with a brown paper bag in his hand.

The edge of somebody's leg, blurred.

Peter had a sense of futility, of having wasted his time.

Then there was one of Elliott, beautifully clear. He was standing in the doorway, one hand raised, as if he were seeing somebody out; there wasn't anybody else in the picture, though. There was a dark spot at the edge, which might have been a shadow.

Two more of the door, darker now as the shadows deepened.

"Terrific stuff," Gunther was saying, whistling in mock appreciation. "I mean, real terrific."

A teenage girl.

Two more of the door.

Half of a cop passing—or at least somebody in uniform.

"You know what?" Gunther said. "You could exhibit these, man. There's always some loony prepared to pay a fortune for stuff he doesn't understand. You could call the exhibition The Edges of Things. You like that?"

"I hate it," Peter said.

Gunther hung up a few more. They were darker.

And then there was a curious one, one so strange that Peter felt something become tight in his chest. It was blurry and indistinct, and the shadows were darker still, but it showed a blonde woman apparently passing the steps. . . .

A blonde with black glasses . . .

Hadn't Marino said something like that?

But then Peter's brief excitement passed. This blonde had no dark glasses, nor was it obvious that she was leaving Elliott's office. Christ, she could be anybody, anybody just passing by in the street. Don't get your hopes up. In any case, the picture was so dark that it was hard to make anything out. What the hell, it was as bad as the other pictures. He clenched his hands in frustration.

Then there were a couple more of the door, now almost totally dark.

"That's it, man. I think you've thrown ten bucks down the tubes," Gunther said.

"Yeah. Looks that way."

"You want them anyhow?"

Peter nodded. "I might as well. I paid for them, didn't I?"

Gunther giggled. "Anytime you need fast work done, Peter, you know I'm your man."

When he left Gunther's Peter cycled to a drugstore. He bought another roll of film, dropped it inside the camera, and rode back to the NO PARKING sign outside Elliott's office. He adjusted the time-lapse control of the small electric motor so that the shutter would start operating just after dawn of the following day, then take a shot every fifteen minutes. Maybe he'd have better luck this time, but it was hard to avoid the feeling he'd begun to entertain that the whole thing was a wild exercise in futility.

He padlocked the bike to the sign, then made sure that the metal box was fastened securely to the rack.

He looked across the street at Elliott's door.

Then he locked the other padlock, the one attached to the box.

When he'd finished, he stared once more across the street.

It was hard to tell—the light was bad, the streetlamps feeble, the exhaust from a passing bus suddenly dense—it was hard to tell anything, but he felt all his pulses leap abruptly; and it was as if something impossibly bright had lit up in the dark of his head.

SIX

1

He was a man in his late thirties, slightly overweight, and he wore bifocal glasses that continually slipped down the bone of his nose, so that he had to keep pushing them back upwards again with a thick index finger. He did this so frequently that it was like a nervous mannerism, a tic he could do nothing to prevent. His clothes were expensively cut, the vest tailored to disguise the plumpness of his belly. He occupied a suite of rooms on the top floor of the Parkway: a large living room with a view of the darkness that was Central Park, a bedroom through whose open door Liz could see a king-size bed. He spoke with the kind of accent that has been processed through good Eastern schools. Across the front of his vest there was a gold watch chain.

When he asked Liz to come in he said, "I assume you're from the escort service—"

"That's right," she said. She went at once to the window and looked out at the blackness of the park far below.

He said, "You're very pretty."

"What did you expect? Quasimodo?"

He laughed. "Hardly that. It's just that sometimes . . . sometimes one's expectations aren't exactly met."

She turned around to look at him, noticing an ice bucket on a table, a bottle of champagne. She was conscious of how he was staring at her, scrutinizing her, as if some set of inner calculations were rushing through his head. He took the bottle of champagne from the bucket and, straining, managed to uncork it. He poured two glasses and handed her one. She sipped it slowly, watching him over the rim of her glass.

"Nice place," she said.

"It costs an arm and a leg," he answered. "Company money."

"What kind of company?"

"Consultancy. The placement of upper echelon personnel. You know, executives, vice-presidents, those kind of people."

"And that's what you do?"

The man smiled. "It's *my* company," he said.

"So you're the company president?"

"President and owner and anything else you'd care to name." He sat down on a sofa. He patted the cushion next to him and Liz walked across the floor, sat beside him, crossed her legs so that her skirt slid upwards, the slit revealing a pale surface of thigh.

"Where do you come from?" he said. "I've been trying to place your accent. Usually I'm quite good at that."

"Chicago, originally," she said.

"Chicago is such a vital place," he said. "I get there a lot."

He paused, twisted the stem of his glass between his fingers, smiled at her. His other hand touched the faint scratch marks on the back of her fingers.

"An accident?" he said.

"A bad-tempered cat," she answered.

"Pity. You have such nice hands." He finished his drink and reached for the bottle again. When he offered it to Liz, she shook her head.

"Were you in the same line of business in Chicago?" he asked.

"I taught remedial reading," Liz said.

"Remedial reading?" He tilted his head back, smiled in an absentminded way. "Forgive the question—how do you get from remedial reading to becoming . . ."

"A hooker?"

"Yes."

"The pay is better."

"Ah, the mercenary motive. I understand that."

Liz put her glass down on the table. "I'll make more money tonight than I'd make in a month of teaching kids. I also tried a little secretarial work before I went into teaching, but I had this boss who wanted to pay me two hundred a week *and* fuck me in the bargain. So I didn't fuck him, which meant I got fired. After a while, you begin to realize you've got your priorities confused. . . ."

The man touched her wrist. "How long have you been in this business?"

She stared at him. "We don't have to talk, you know."

"I'm enjoying it," he said.

"It's your bread." She looked at her watch. "And I hate to mention it, but your meter is running."

"Company money," the man said. "My name's Sam, by the way."

Liz leaned her head back against the sofa. *A talker.* Why did so many of them want to talk? Speech was the lowest form of aphrodisiac. She'd had people in the past who bought her time out of some terrible loneliness, people who had no intention of screwing: the lonely conventioneers, businessmen, sad salesmen. Some of them even dragged out photographs of wife and family for your perusal, and you made suitably impressed noises. Now he was filling his glass again.

"Are you married?" she asked.

"Eight years."

"Have you cheated on your wife before?"

"Cheated?" He looked a little perplexed. "This doesn't really count as cheating, does it?"

"Why not?"

"Well . . . I mean, you're a professional."

"Which means I'm not a woman—"

"Hey, I didn't mean anything like that—"

"You're a little mixed-up, Sam, I think. No matter how you cut it, this is cheating."

"Yeah, but it's not cheating in a classical sense."

Liz turned her face away from him. There was something slightly delectable in springing a little morality where it was least expected. Call girl with portable pulpit. *All ye that cheat and are heavy-laden, give yourselves to me. . . .* She looked back at him seeing how flustered he appeared now, as if his uneasiness were yielding to guilt. Carry on like this, Liz, she thought, and you'll be out of business in a flash. She reached over and took his hand, which was cold and heavy, like some hairless paw. Then she stood up and walked inside the bedroom, where she

started to undress. She could hear him pour another glass
of champagne and gulp it down hastily. Naked, she lay
down on the bed and waited. After a moment he appeared in the doorway, undoing the buttons of his vest
and removing the gold watch chain, which he draped,
rather carelessly, over the back of a chair. He slipped out
of his jacket and shirt, undid the suspenders of his pants,
and stood there—like some white whale taught to remain
erect on its tail, a zoo trick—in his boxer shorts, which
were polka-dotted and too tight round his midriff. Close
your eyes, she thought. Close your eyes and smile and
open your arms in welcome.

She heard him pad towards the bed. The mattress
sagged as he slumped beside her. She felt his wet lips
upon the side of her neck and she wondered, as she'd
wondered before too many times, whether the price was
worth it after all, whether the memory of this encounter
and of all similar ones would finally fade from her mind
at some later point.

"You're very beautiful," he was saying.

His entrance was something short of dramatic. She
made a brief gasping sound and threw her arms around
his neck, the tips of her fingers tracing the ridged outline
of his spine.

2

When she left the hotel the night had become chilly, a
dark wind blowing across the great wasteland of the park,
rustling dying leaves and shaking branches. She turned up
the collar of her coat and shivered on the sidewalk. A
cab—where was a cab when you needed one? She looked
at the uniformed doorman of the hotel: He was staring at
her with the kind of suspicion you'd expect on a cop's
face, as if in his mind he were accusing her of unspeak-
able transgressions. Flunkey, she thought, wondering if
she looked like a hooker, if there was something about
her that made the antennae of such people as doormen
quiver. Then she saw a cab cruising down the other side of
the street and she hailed it, watching it swing in a leisure-
ly arc to the sidewalk. The driver was young, fresh-faced,
probably a college kid working nights.

As she reached forward to the door, something made her glance across the street.

A dark car. A movement, the reflection of light as the car door was opened. Quick, blinding, like some visual hallucination.

A dark car and a blonde woman getting inside it.

She stepped inside the taxi, slamming the door, leaning forward to the driver. For a moment she didn't say anything; when she turned her face she saw the dark car's headlights go on, the car itself pulling away slowly from the sidewalk.

The driver turned his face, looking puzzled. "Where to, lady?"

Liz couldn't think. Blankness. A total emptiness of mind.

"I don't have all night," the driver said.

Liz watched the car, then looked at the driver. "I know how this is going to sound, and I'm sorry if you think you just picked up a loony, but somebody is following me."

"Huh?"

"That car. Just there."

The driver twisted his neck round, then shook his head. "*That* car?"

"Yeah. The black one."

"I believe you. Don't ask me why—"

"Don't ask anything. Just lose it, huh?"

The driver pulled the cab away from the sidewalk so abruptly that Liz fell backwards in her seat. When she turned to look again through the rear window she could see the car a little way behind, following at a steady pace. She swung round and leaned forward towards the driver, speaking to him through the glass partition.

"Can't you go a little faster?"

"I can try," the kid said, wheeling the cab suddenly around a corner, wheeling it so hard that the tires screamed against the concrete. Liz held on, trying to think. It doesn't matter how she found me, it doesn't matter how she knew where to look, the only important thing now is to lose her. But when she turned around once again the dark car was still there, doggedly, still the same short distance behind.

"And screw the red lights," Liz said.

"Anything you say," the driver said.

Now they were in the middle of some heavy uptown traffic, the cab weaving around a bus at such a sharp angle that Liz slipped from her seat to the floor.

"You okay?" the kid asked.

"Apart from a couple of fractures, sure . . ."

"How am I doing?"

"You're doing just great. But that car's doing just as great."

"Fuck it," the driver said. He swung the wheel hard, the cab made a breakneck left turn, the rear tires climbing the edge of the sidewalk then bumping back down again. "Sorry about that."

"It doesn't matter," Liz said.

"What kinda trouble you got anyhow?"

"That would take too long to explain," Liz said, turning again, watching the other car stream through traffic to keep the yellow cab in sight.

"You know the subway at Columbus Circle?" Liz said.

"Yeah. You want out there?"

"Drop me at the station—"

"You think that's wise?"

"I stopped thinking wise a while back," Liz said.

The kid swung his vehicle again, rushing through a bunch of frightened pedestrians who were crossing at a WALK sign. Liz saw a blurred group of faces back away in surprise and anger. *Fucking cabbies think they own the city!*

The driver looked in his rearview mirror. "The goddamn thing's still there," he said. Then Liz saw him glance at her, a slight look of approval flick across his eyes. "Listen, if I get you outta this, how about a date some time?"

"You get me out of this, you got more than a date," Liz said. She looked at his nameplate in the front compartment, the black and white photograph staring sullenly out. Eric Spellman, the name said.

"All *right*," the kid said, pumping the gas harder, bumping over intersections, scattering pedestrians and ignoring stop lights.

"I got your name," Liz said. "I'll call you."

"I'll look forward to it."

Liz turned again. The goddamn car—why couldn't they get rid of it? It was there, dogging them like some persistent hound, like something predatory that wouldn't let go of a spoor.

"Drop me here," she said. "I'll make it to the subway."

She fumbled some money from her purse, and passed it to the driver without counting it out.

"You sure you want to get out here?" he asked.

"Yeah—" And she opened the door, running towards the subway entrance, turning once to see the black car pull in to the sidewalk behind the parked cab. The door opened and the blonde woman hurried along the sidewalk —just as Eric Spellman, bless him, *bless him,* opened the door of his cab and caught the woman as she was passing, the edge of the door striking her in the stomach, winding her, winding her so badly that she clutched her stomach and sank to her knees.

Liz didn't stop to see any more.

She rushed inside the subway entrance, bought a token, and headed for the trains.

For the first time since she'd left the hotel she felt secure, but the security was a flimsy thing, because behind it there lay a darker question she couldn't answer—

How did she know where to find me?

And if she can find me once . . .

3

Beep.

She held the receiver, waited, sighed deeply into it.

You know what I did with your razor, hotshot? You know by now, don't you? I expect you'll tell the heat, huh? What'll you say, Elliott? One of my patients, I beg your pardon, former *patients, broke into my office and took my razor and I think she used it, oh dear me, as the murder weapon. . . . Good heavens, what is the world coming to, Doc? Want to know something neat? I went out and I got myself a brand new razor, real nice it is, pearl handle and beautiful clean blade. . . . You see, there was this girl, and she saw me with Kate Myers in*

*the elevator . . . You should have been there. Still. She saw
me, you understand that? You know what I have to do
now? Say, Doc, how are you going to put a stop to me?
Maybe you could call Levy and tell him it's okay for me
to have the operation, huh? Maybe that way I wouldn't
have to kill again. Such power. What does it feel like,
Elliott, to have such power? What the fuck, I don't give a
shit for you. . . . Read about me in the papers tomorrow,
Doc. Okay?*

She hung up, stepped out of the telephone booth.

The night air had a quality of ice to it.

Liz climbed the subway steps, pausing when she
reached the street, feeling far beneath her the vibration of
wheels on a track. She stared across the street, looking
towards the entranceway to her apartment building. *Why
do I hesitate like this?*

Fear.

She found me once. . . .

*But you lost her near the station at Columbus Circle,
didn't you?*

*All you have to do now is get upstairs to your apart-
ment, lock yourself in, call Marino and tell him what
happened.*

That's all.

She shuddered as the wind, smelling of frost, of dreary
winter, sliced through her coat, played against the surface
of her leg that was visible between the slit in her
dress.

Scared shitless.

*But so far as you know she's still back at Columbus
Circle, somewhere, maybe hunting faces along the platform, maybe looking for you.*

Hell. She couldn't find me now.

Still she didn't move from the top of the steps. A
subway smell, dank and airless, drifted up from below.
She stared at the apartment building again. She gazed up
at the windows seeing the darkened glass of her own
apartment.

Move, she told herself.

Cross the street. You're safe now.

For a moment she couldn't catch her breath. It was as if her lungs had become constricted, shrivelled, useless sacs in her ribcage. Nerves, hypertension. What was the cure for that—didn't you have to breath into a paper bag or something? Fill your lungs with carbon dioxide or whatever it was called.

She still didn't move. It was as if she were conscious of being watched, of something out there in the darkened street, something that—when she thought about it, about its lack of shape, its absence of identity—made her dizzy. She leaned against the wall. From below there were more vibrations, trains whining in the blackness of tunnels, like vehicles rushing nowhere.

She stepped away from the wall, walked to the edge of the sidewalk, wondered why the appearance of the apartment building was suddenly so menacing, like something created to entice her forward, a trap, a snare. But it's stupid, she thought, it's ridiculous, you lost the woman at Columbus Circle, you're home and dry now....

Home free.

She stepped off the edge of the sidewalk.

There was a loud report, an echo from somewhere, a noise that might have been gunfire but which was the sound of a car backfiring. The noise cut through her. She turned her head in the direction it came from. She saw nothing. She saw only a telephone booth, a shadow pressed against the glass of the box. The shadow moved, moved as though it were incorporeal, attached to nothing substantial.

It emerged from the box.

It came out, frozen for a moment beneath a pale streetlamp, frozen and still like an old photograph. The dark glasses were perched, in the manner of a black gash, above the frigid smile. The blonde hair caught the streetlamp in a suggestion of flame.

Jesus—

Liz didn't move for a moment.

I lost you at Columbus Circle, she thought. The thought, absurdly, repeated itself in her mind like a tired old echo. I lost you at Columbus Circle. Columbuscircle—

The figure stepped forward from the box.

Run, Liz thought. Turn and run, just fucking run.

Something glinted in the figure's hand, flashing in the pale lamp suspended overhead.

Dear God, make yourself run—

She wheeled round, found herself dashing down the steps of the subway entrance, running and not looking back but hearing the echoes of footsteps anyhow.

A toll booth.

A token.

A turnstile.

It clicked stiffly as she shoved her way through.

Run. Just run. Questions. They don't need answers.

She found you. Wherever you go, she finds you.

Breathless, her heart knocking against rib bones, her blood screaming, she rushed along the platform. Where now? Where? There was nobody on the platform except for five black guys at the far end, and she thought: Safety in numbers. Safety in a crowd. She walked quickly towards the group and then, as she reached it, she turned and looked back along the platform. No sign of the blonde woman, nothing, like it was something she'd dreamed. Call it hysteria. An hysterical reaction. The dying man in the desert sees the oasis inverted in the sky. The scared person dreams his own fears.

"Look at this, look at what we got *here*," one of the guys said. He was wearing a full-length fur coat and a hat with a brightly colored band from which a feather protruded. He flashed a white smile.

Liz stared at their faces. Behind the smiles there was something sullen, something dangerous, a menace barely hidden.

"Hey lady what you lookin' for down here, huh?" another said, shuffling around Liz, clicking his fingers together.

"A train," Liz said. "What else?"

"A train, huh?"

Now they were all circling her, smiling in that same menacing fashion, and she felt dizzy again.

"Hey, Jack, you're the guy really digs this white meat, ain't you?"

The one called Jack looked sulky a moment. "I like to

break ass, brother. I like to see them little old white faces down there gobbling at my pork."

They laughed, still circling her. She remembered an old saying that concerned the difference between frying pans and fires. She glanced back along the platform again. Nothing. One of the guys pushed her lightly on the shoulder.

"She ain't bad looking all right," somebody said.

"Break ass or fuck her, I ain't exactly giving a shit," another said.

Liz stepped away from the circle. At the far end of the desolate platform she saw the blonde woman appear.

"We was standing here minding our business, lady. What right you got coming along and interr-*upteeng* a private conversation? You wanna learn some manners cunt?"

"Hey, look," Liz said.

"I am *looking*," one of them said. "What am I meant to see?"

"That woman down there—"

"I don't see no woman—"

"Her. The blonde."

"Yeah. So what? What's it signify, lady?"

"I saw her kill a woman—"

A couple of them laughed. "She killed somebody, huh? Well, fuck that. You call the cops, lady?"

"I don't exactly see any, do you?"

"Damn right I don't see any," one of them said. He had a leather cap which he removed, inverted, looked inside; then he scratched his hair. "I'm gonna tell you something, lady. Supposin' I did see the heat, supposin' the fuckin' heat was standin' right next to me, I wouldn't bust my balls to tell him about no goddamn murder, no way."

"Sheeit," the one called Jack said. He hawked and spat on the platform, smearing the mucus with the sole of his shoe. "I got it in mind to fuck you, lady. Know that?"

Liz stared back down the platform. The blonde was watching her. There, at the far end of the platform, beneath a shabby pale light, she was watching, the light creating a faint nimbus around her head. The angel of death. The guy called Jack grabbed her by the arm and brought his face close to hers, so close his lips brushed against her own.

"Yeah, I got it in mind to fuck you bad," he said.

She shook her arm free and he laughed, shuffling from side to side. He moved like some kind of dilapidated prizefighter while the others circled round him as though it were all a ritual whose meaning she couldn't understand, but underneath it she knew there was violence. She could feel the tense little currents of violence run between them like filaments ready to explode inside a lightbulb. Once more she turned and stared down the platform. The blonde hadn't moved. She was still staring. Motionless, staring. Liz looked towards the darkness of the tunnel. Maybe she could jump down onto the tracks and head for the tunnel, but that struck her as being senseless, trapped in blackness, waiting for the scream of a train to come through. She shut her eyes a moment. Think. Think your way out of this one, baby. She was having trouble breathing, as if the air were rancid and poisonous, air trapped too long below ground.

Jack was holding her by the arm again, pulling her towards him.

"You ain't so bad to look at," he said. The others, milling around him, were laughing. How could they laugh? Why didn't they believe her about the blonde? It wouldn't matter even if they did believe her, because she understood they didn't care.

"You ain't so bad at all," Jack said again.

She pulled her arm from him and stared back down the tunnel, watching the blackness as if her only real solution lay there. Fear, fear reduced you to a place where you couldn't think, where you couldn't get anything straight in your mind and everything was a jumble, everything the result of some panic button that had been pressed. *Think, goddamnit, think of something.* There wasn't even a transit cop around. She was alone on this godforsaken platform with five black guys and a maniac.

"Sheeit," Jack said. He nudged her with his elbow. "You and me, we could go over there, get it on—"

"Fuck off," she said.

Down the platform the blonde moved slightly, almost

imperceptibly, like a hunter who knows the meaning of patience, of waiting for the quarry to be alone.

"Fuck off, you hear the lady? Fuck off, Jack," one of them said, slapping his hands together, laughing.

"I don't believe what my ears is telling me," Jack said. "You say that was impolite? Ladies don't talk like that."

Liz moved a few paces away. They came after her. The blonde also moved, a couple of steps. A sandwich, Liz thought. A goddamn sandwich. Then there was a rumbling sound and the light of a train appeared in the tunnel. She moved further away from them as the train slithered into the platform. She rushed towards it just as it ground to a halt and the doors popped open. She stepped inside. The car was empty except for a sleeping drunk in a stained raincoat who clutched a brown paper bag between his slack hands. She heard the doors slide shut and the train begin to move and she slumped into a seat, turning her face towards the glass door of the adjoining car. Oh fuck, sweet suffering fuck.

They were there in the next car, their faces pressed against the glass. They looked grotesque, their noses and lips flattened upon glass. Quickly she got up and walked down the car away from them, swaying as the train took a bend, reaching for a strap to remain upright. The drunk mumbled something as she walked past him, then shifted his position and the paper bag fell, spilling a half-empty bottle on the floor. She reached the end of the car, paused, turned around. They had come through the door into the car, laughing, calling after her.

"Grab that cunt! Grab that cocksucking cunt!"

Shaking, she stopped at the door of the next car down, feeling the train sway again, feeling it vibrate underneath her. She hauled on the handle. The damn thing was hard to twist. She strained, sweating, trying to get it open.

"Hey cunt! Where you think you going?"

She opened the door and stepped into space, into darkness, poised between the two cars, feeling the dank wind tear through her hair, flash through her clothes, feeling it climb up through the slit in her skirt. Dear Christ, where now? The next car. You can't go back. You can't stay here. She looked down, seeing streamers of track reflected dully in the lights from the cars. When they reach you they'll throw you down on the track. Story ended. *Finis*. She shut her eyes as the wind sucked at her, ripped at her, as though it were determined to draw her off the train and down into the wheels.

She opened the door of the next car down, vaguely conscious of the bright graffiti that decorated the interior of the car like paint sprayed by madmen. The car was empty. Jesus Christ. Why wasn't there somebody around? Why wasn't there somebody who could help her? She rushed down the length of the car, losing a shoe, turning once to see them coming through the door, still chasing after her.

"You can't run much further, cunt!"

She reached the door of the next car down, pulled it open, and found herself back in that same black space as before, the dark wind howling against her, her skirt blown up around her waist, the wind blistering her eyes.

And then she slipped.

She slipped, stumbled, blown off balance, hanging for a terrifying moment just above the track, the wheels grating so loud the sound seemed to be inside her. The savage grinding that appeared to originate inside her head. She clawed herself back upright, fumbled with the catch of the connecting door, stepped inside the car and stood for a moment with her back against the door. Her heart, her pulses—they were things about to explode. She shut her eyes, tried to catch her breath, tried to reassemble her senses. But there was no time. There was no time to stop. In a moment they would come through the door into this car and she'd have to run again and she wondered how much further she could go, when she would reach the last car.

And after that—

She opened her eyes.

The car was empty except for the blonde.

The blonde.

For a moment Liz couldn't move. Caught. Stuck. Paralyzed. She wanted to scream aloud but whatever sound she might have made froze inside her, congealed in a silent lump at the back of her throat. The blonde was grinning behind the huge dark glasses. The elevator, the blood, the dead woman's fingers scratching the back of her hand.... She turned, looked back at the connecting door, saw the five black guys come slowly through. It was a place beyond fear now, as if whatever sensations she might have felt had gone to a point where language was useless. She had a feeling of something coming to an end, a curtain falling, a sense of nothingness. A person drowning, she thought, is said to go through stages, the first struggle, then the futile acceptance, then the final transcendental moment of death....

A person drowning.

She stared at the blonde. Then she looked at the black guys as they came slowly down the car. She moved, so that she had her back to the double doors, thinking in a panic of an emergency exit, of clawing those automatic doors open, falling out into the darkness of the tracks, maybe hurting herself bad, but not dying, maybe having a chance. Then she thought about saying to the guys: *That woman, she's the one I told you about, she's the killer, she wants to kill me....*

They'd laugh.

They'd just goddamn laugh.

Fight, she thought. With what? What have you got to fight with?

She glanced at the blonde. That same manic grin. That dreadful expression. The elevator...

Then she felt the train slowing, she felt the pressure of brakes being applied, and she was conscious of the lights of a platform beginning to slice through the dark of the tunnel. She turned her head towards the five guys. Then she looked around for the blonde.

But the woman was gone.

Where?

"Grab that cocksucker!"

She felt the doors pop open behind her, but she couldn't get herself to move, couldn't get herself to step backwards off the train and on to the platform. This goddamn fear, this paralysis—

She shut her eyes.

When she opened them she saw, as in a dream, the five guys backing slowly away, turning, moving as if they'd seen something they didn't want to see, something they didn't want to be involved in. For a moment, Liz didn't understand. And then she turned her head.

From behind, from the platform, the razor was falling.

It fell in a blinding rainbow of steel.

She could hear it slash the air as it dropped, slicing, whistling, carving space.

She turned her head to the side, eyes shut, one hand raised to ward off the blow—

It didn't come. It didn't happen.

Instead, she heard the blonde woman gasp. And when she opened her eyes she saw the woman cover her face with her hands, the face itself a mess of foam, of white froth, a coating that looked like lather.

Liz backed on to the platform.

She watched the blonde woman rush along the platform, her hands pressed to her face still, and then she was conscious of a kid, a boy of about fifteen, standing alongside her with an aerosol can in his hand. She stared at him, puzzled, then her strength went, whatever muscle control she had disintegrated, and she had to lean against a pillar, watching the kid stuff the can inside the satchel he carried.

She closed her eyes, wanting to cry from relief, vaguely conscious of the train doors closing and the wheels beginning to roll out of the station.

Dear God, she thought. That razor falling . . .

The kid said, "The stuff won't kill her. Just enough to blind her for a time, that's all. Just enough to sting her."

Liz opened her eyes. "Start at the beginning, kid. Start at the beginning and give it to me slowly in a way I can understand."

The boy swung his satchel over his shoulder and grinned at her. "My mother was Kate Myers. And that woman killed her."

4

They sat in a diner, Peter toying with a large sundae, Liz sipping tasteless coffee and smoking a cigarette. She couldn't keep her hands from shaking, couldn't still the sense of inner turmoil she felt. Even when she raised the coffee cup to her lips, slicks of the brown liquid overflowed into the saucer. She watched the boy spoon a heap of vanilla ice cream into his mouth, casually, almost as if nothing had happened.

"So you rigged up this camera thing?" Liz said.

Peter nodded. "Yeah. But the results were pretty bad. I'll show you them in a minute. Anyhow, I was setting the camera up again when I saw her across the street. She was coming down the steps from Elliott's office, and I remembered that cop, what's his name . . . ?"

"Marino?"

"Marino. I remembered him describing the woman you saw in the elevator. He described her to Elliott, but Elliott didn't seem to know her."

"Which means what?"

"Which means he's protecting a patient—" Peter looked a little exasperated, as if the woman's slowness were inexcusable.

"Why would he do something like that?" Liz asked. She stared at the kid, liking him, amused by the little glint of intensity in the dark eyes behind the glasses.

Peter shrugged. "They're like priests, shrinks. I mean, they don't just go round giving confidential stuff away, do they?"

Liz stubbed her cigarette. She looked for a moment round the diner. Two waitresses were standing at the cash register, giggling conspiratorially over something.

"Yeah, okay," she said. "But what if it comes down to a killer? I mean, is he going to save a killer's ass?"

"It looks that way," Peter said. He dug his straw into the remains of the sundae, making a slurping sound. "The next step is to find out that blonde's name. Which shouldn't be too hard, if I can get a look at Elliott's appointments book—"

"Hey, kid. You ever hear about the cops? I mean, that's something they should be doing, not you."

"They don't act fast enough for me," Peter said.

Liz was quiet for a moment. "Forgive the observation, Peter, but you're just a kid—"

"A kid that happened to save your life!"

"Point taken," Liz said. "So what are you going to do?

Burst into the guy's office? Steal his precious appointments book?"

Peter stared inside his empty sundae glass. "I'm not sure yet. I'll think of something."

Liz smiled at him and leaned forward, lightly touching the back of his hand. The gesture seemed to embarrass him and he blushed.

"I saw you at the precinct house," he said. "I watched you go through the mug shots."

"You're quite a little spy, aren't you?"

"I get around," Peter said. "When she left Elliott's office, I trailed her. She led me straight to you. . . ."

Liz lit another cigarette. She was thinking about the woman she'd lost at Columbus Circle, she was remembering the relief she felt, the relief that crumbled when the blonde emerged from the telephone booth. How could the goddamn woman have found her so quickly? But that question was eclipsed by another one, a more important one. And she looked at Peter, asking, "The thing that troubles me is how did she know where to find me? How does she know where I live, for God's sake?"

"I don't know," Peter said.

"I don't know either, but it doesn't take a genius to figure out that my apartment isn't exactly the safest place in the world right now."

"So where will you go?"

"I'll check into a hotel or something, just for tonight. Then I'll call Marino first thing in the morning—"

"Do it now," Peter said.

"All I want to do now is sleep, kid."

"Sleep. Sleep's a real waste of time. . . ."

"When you reach my advanced years, you begin to realize its tonic effects, Peter. Believe me." She patted the back of his hand again, and this time, smiling shyly, he looked around the diner to see if anybody had noticed the touch. Then he took his hand away and reached inside his satchel. He took out the blurry photograph of the blonde woman and slid it across the table to Liz. She picked it up, studied it, shuddered.

"If I had to put money on it, I'd say that was our lady," she said. "It's not exactly clear, but it's good enough."

She handed the picture back.

She was quiet for a time, then she said, "You're a pretty smart kid, Peter. I didn't see you on the train. All I can say is thank Christ you were there at the right moment. With that spray stuff of yours—"

"Oh, that. I made it myself. I'm too young to carry a gun around even if I wanted to, but I feel pretty safe with the aerosol."

"You made it *yourself?*"

"Sure. It's a derivative of orthochlorobenzalmalononitrile—"

"If I tried to say that I'd choke to death on the first couple of syllables. Whatever it is, it saved my little ass. I owe you one."

"You don't owe me anything. But you *could* go to the cops tonight. You could call Marino right now—"

"Hey, a little patience goes a long way. And the funny thing about fear, as I'm beginning to find out, is when the adrenaline fades, you feel totally hollowed out, wasted. You know what I mean?"

Peter, looking disappointed, nodded.

"Cheer up, kid," she said. "I'll try the cops first thing in the morning, and if that doesn't pan out, we'll dream up something else—just you and me." She pushed her empty coffee cup away, crushed her cigarette out. "You want to share a taxi with me? I can drop you off."

Peter looked hesitant. "Well . . ."

"Well what?"

"The thing is, I told my stepfather I was staying the night with a friend, because we were supposed to be working on a science project together . . ."

"And you want me to cover for you, right?"

Peter smiled. "Right."

"You want to share a hotel room with me? Right?"

"Right." The kid fidgeted with the edge of the ashtray. "It would also help me a whole lot if you didn't mention my name to the cops when you talk with them. Mike would find out that I'd lied to him . . . and I don't think the results would be pleasant. At least, not the way he is now."

"Okay," she said, rising, reaching out to ruffle his hair.

He thought: My mother used to do that, she used to do that in the same way.

"I'll keep your name out of it, kid. Don't worry."

They went towards the door, which Peter held open for her.

"I've checked into hotels with some strange people in my time," she said, stepping past him, shivering in the dark city wind. "But this is a first for me—a fifteen-year-old kid."

She went to the edge of the sidewalk and hailed a passing cab, half-expecting the door to open and the grinning blonde woman to be sitting, razor raised, inside.

5

Elliott had gone out to dinner, eating alone in a nearby restaurant. When he returned to his office he switched on his answering machine, listening to Bobbi's voice, listening only to a fraction of the message before he turned the thing off . . . *Say, Doc, how are you going to put a stop to me . . . ?* He wanted to break the machine, destroy it, so he wouldn't have to listen to that ghastly voice any more.

He felt scared. It wasn't an emotion to which he was accustomed. He didn't know how to deal with it, and it was accentuated in some way by the curious loneliness he felt, the riveting emptiness of his office, the strangely flat appearance of the objects within the room, as if half-lost in shadows they had shed a dimension. He rubbed his eyes. He sat for a time on the sofa, his hands pressed flat against his face.

Then he got up and walked to the telephone, dialled his home number, and waited for Anne to answer. This loneliness, he thought. This cutting fear . . . Why couldn't he fight it back?

He heard her voice. She sounded slightly drunk, or maybe it was the effect of her sleeping pills.

"It's late," she said. "Why are you calling so late?"

"I'd like to come home," he said. He glanced at the half-open door of his bathroom. Something inside, something vague and indistinct, caught his attention. He wasn't sure what.

"This isn't your home any more, my dear," she said. "I thought I'd made that clear—"

"Wait," he said. "I think we could talk this thing over, don't you? I think we could work something out."

"There are times, love, when I really believe you live in a dream. What you're suggesting is quite impossible. Don't you know that? We're through. Finished. It's *done*."

The loneliness was oceanic, tidal, pressing in on him now. The walls of his office smothered him.

"Listen, Anne," he said. "I could come home now. I could be there in an hour or so. I think we have one or two things to talk over—"

"Damn you, damn you. We haven't got anything to talk over!"

He was silent, staring again at the bathroom door, sensing the edge of some presence, something that shouldn't have been there.

She lowered her voice to a whisper. "Besides, I have company."

"Company?"

"You heard me."

"Who?" He could hardly force the question out. There was a thickness at the back of his throat. And he wondered if what he felt was the quickening of some odd jealousy. How could that be?

"It doesn't matter who—"

"A man?"

"A man, yes."

Elliott, holding the receiver still, stretching the cord, moved around his desk and pushed the bathroom door open with his foot. *Something*. He couldn't reach the light switch.

"Somebody you sleep with?" he asked.

"Somebody I'm about to sleep with, my dear."

"God."

"I hope your sofa is comfortable, darling."

Click. Dead. Hung up.

He slammed the receiver down and stood in the thresh-

hold of the darkened bathroom. He didn't know why he
was afraid to turn the light on.

And then he caught it.

A faint scent. A lingering perfume that was familiar to
him.

He fumbled for the light switch.

He found himself staring at the mirror.

Then he closed his eyes and leaned against the door
jamb.

How had she got in? How had she managed to enter
the office when he was out? A stolen key?

He looked at the mirror again, seeing the lipsticked
words spread across his own pallid reflection.

SORRY I MISSED YOU DOC BUT I'LL BE
SEEING YOU SOON
LOVE FROM BOBBI

He ripped several squares of toilet tissue from the roll
and began feverishly to wipe at the words. But the more
he worked the more the writing smeared so that the whole
mirror was soon a mass of red streaks. He crumpled the
tissue and dropped it in the toilet, then stepped back. She
was here when I was out, he thought. Here.

He slammed the bathroom door and went to the sofa,
where he lay down with his eyes shut. Tomorrow, he
thought, he would see Levy. After that, he couldn't go on
protecting Bobbi.

How could he?

SEVEN

1

The weather changed. The clear skies became muddy, storm clouds hung across the city with the inevitability of some unnameable doom, shrouding the peaks of high-rise buildings in a dark mist. Marino, stepping out of his parked car, looked up at the sky. This wasn't his kind of weather. He reacted to it in a personal way, disliking it as he might detest an enemy. It brought on dull headaches and caused his sinuses to ache. He walked across the parking lot and went inside the precinct house. He'd slept badly last night, dreaming distorted dreams, haunted by unidentifiable shapes. Once, when he'd woken up sweating, his skin adhering to the bedsheets, Mary had propped herself up on an elbow and stroked his forehead. *You're coming down with something, Joseph. You really need to take better care of yourself.* But now he wasn't sure if he'd dreamed that up either; and when he'd left the house that morning she was still asleep, so he couldn't ask her to be sure. Funny that—how you sometimes had to check reality out, confirming events with other people.

He went inside his office and hung his coat up on the wall. He sat behind his desk and reached for the tickets to the ball game. Shit, he thought. I can't break that promise. He stuck the tickets inside his jacket pocket, then he thought about the Myers killing. It was like a surface of hard ice without a crack in sight. What did he have except for Liz Blake? And that didn't amount to a big score. He could hardly drag her in and book her without something a little more solid to go on, and besides, he couldn't think of a motive that would explain Liz Blake killing Kate Myers. So what did he have? A great fucking blind alley. Okay, what about the shrink? What about one of the shrink's patients? Straws in the wild wind. Sometimes, though, you had to clutch what you could. He stared, deep in thought, at the surface of his desk.

Messages, messages.

At three A.M. that morning a body had been fished out of the river up around 125th Street. Marino read the report, skimming it. *Female caucasian. Dead for roughly three days. Multiple stab wounds.* Multiple stab wounds, for Christ's sake.

At four thirty-seven A.M. a corpse had been found in a derelict tenement. *Black male, age approximately forty, gunshot wounds to the face and neck.*

He put the reports aside and stood up, strolled to the window, looked out. What was it about the human race that made it want to self-destruct? What kind of mad genetic factor was it that caused people to kill? He pressed his face against the glass. The city doesn't pay you to be a philosopher, he thought. It pays you to solve these fucking murders, and when you don't, the taxpayers have a tendency to become irate. Somebody like Kate Myers lies in a bath of her own blood—shit, the taxpayer wants to be sure that he isn't going to be the next goddamn victim.

The door of his office opened.

He turned to see a uniformed cop standing there. A new guy, fresh uniform, a look of eagerness about the eyes. After a while, that kind of light was extinguished, and what you saw instead was a glazed weariness.

"Yeah?" Marino said.

"There's somebody to see you, sir," the young cop said.

"Who?"

"A Miss Blake."

Marino raised his eyebrows, then nervously touched the edge of his moustache. "I'll see her," he said.

The young cop went out. Then Liz Blake came in.

Marino indicated she should sit, but she didn't. She stood with her hands in the pockets of her coat, her face pale and tired. A hard night's work, Marino thought. It had to be a hell of a way to make a few bucks.

"You come down to confess?" he asked.

"How did you guess?" she said.

"Call it a cop's instinct."

She was silent for a time, chewing lightly on her lower lip, her eyes turned towards the window.

"Shitty weather," Marino said.

She nodded. Then she sat down, took a Kleenex from her pocket, and lightly touched the tip of her nose with it. "Something bad happened last night," she said.

"Oh yeah?"

"She tried to kill me."

Marino leaned against the edge of his desk. "Who tried to kill you?"

"The same woman . . . the same woman I saw in the elevator."

"Where did this happen?"

"In the subway—"

"The subway, huh?"

"Do I detect disbelief in your voice, Lieutenant?"

"You imagine too much, Liz."

"You think I imagined I was almost killed? Jesus Christ! She came at me with this razor—"

"Another razor, huh? She must have quite a supply—"

"You don't believe me, is that it?"

"Let's see. A subway. A public place. It stands to reason there must have been a witness, right? It's common enough to find people in subways, as I understand it. . . ."

She looked at him with irritation. "Look, she followed me, I thought I'd lost her, but then she was waiting for me when I got back to my apartment. . . ."

Marino clasped his hands together, moving his arms as if he were swinging an imaginary baseball bat. "I was asking about witnesses. Were there any?"

She paused a moment. "No," she said.

"Terrific, Liz. All kinds of things seem to happen to you when there's nobody else around to see them."

"I didn't come here to listen to your wiseass comments, Marino."

"Marino now. We're getting pretty familiar. Next thing you know we'll be having cocktails in some quiet little bar of an evening."

"Goddamnit, somebody is trying to kill me, Marino—"

"I know a neat little cell where you'll be perfectly safe."

She paused, rose from her chair, went to the window.

Marino watched her. A pretty thing, he thought. What makes a pretty thing like her become a hooker?

Rain was beginning to slither down the window now.

"I'm going to tell you something, Marino. I'm going to tell you how to find this killer."

"I'm all ears," Marino said.

She turned to look at him. "The woman who killed Kate Myers, the same woman who tried to kill me, is a patient of a certain Dr. Elliott."

"So how do you figure that one?"

"She came out of his office."

"You saw her, did you? You just happened to be passing the guy's office when, lo and fucking behold, there she was?"

"I'm getting pretty pissed off with your attitude, Marino."

He shrugged. "Did you see her or didn't you?"

"Not personally, no. But I know she's one of his patients. And all you've got to do is take a look at his appointments book for yesterday and find a name, the rest shouldn't be too hard. Even for you."

"The vote of confidence is appreciated," he said, bowing his head in a mocking way. "Tell you a funny thing, though. I beat you to the punch, sweetheart. I already thought about the good doctor's book, but I just can't walk into his office and pilfer the goddamn thing, because I need a warrant and sometimes a warrant is a slow process because judges have to be wakened from their beauty sleep, which often they don't appreciate. Understand? A cop can't go snooping round a shrink's office without a certain piece of paper."

"That's just wonderful," Liz said. "So while you're wasting your time thinking about this shitty piece of paper, there's a maniac running around—"

"According to you there is," he said.

Liz sighed, irritated. "You don't believe me even yet, do you?"

"Let's just say I'm having this difficulty, Liz. Let's just say there's a credibility gap the size of the Grand Canyon—"

She put her hands firmly on her hips and stared at him. "You know what I think, Marino? I think you're a goddamn incompetent sonofabitch. I think you're what is called a waste of the taxpayer's money, you know that? I'm laying this thing dead in your lap and you're acting like you don't even hear me. . . ."

Marino smiled at her. "Compliments you can save, sweetheart. Right now I'm speculating on how long you'll get. A good lawyer could maybe get you off with twenty—"

"Eat it."

"Or you could be looking at something longer. Life? Hard to tell. Courts work in funny ways, you know." He picked up some papers from his desk, shuffled them, sighed. Then he stared at her again, still smiling in that irksome way. "You're pretty. You're a real good-looking woman. You wouldn't have any trouble finding company in the slammer. I mean, they'd be fighting over proprietorial rights to you, you know that?"

"Marino . . ."

"Naturally, you'd lose some of that bloom you have right now. You'd lose your looks after a time. You'd find yourself walking up and down your thirty-six square feet night after night. And when that old moon comes up through the bars, well . . . Jesus, it'd drive you crazy. Then you'd grow old before your name even came up before the parole board. You'd grow old and hard and pale and you wouldn't be the pretty thing you are now. Tough shit. But sometimes you have to play the cards you're dealt, you know?"

"Spare me the sermons, Marino. You can't book me—"

"Can you stop me, Liz?" He sighed, an actor in an amateur production. He threw his hands up in a play at despair. "You're my main man. You're my numero uno, kid. You're the only ace in my deck, so you better believe I can book you."

She folded her arms and tried to look defiant; but there was something in his eyes, a hard light, a warning, that made her feel small inside, small and frightened.

"Lady, you'd hate jail, believe me. You'd hate the guards, the lack of sunlight, the food that makes you

want to gag. I'd hazard a guess you'd even hate the only
kind of screwing that'd be available to you." He got up
from his desk, stuck his hands in the pockets of his pants,
the smile still on his face. He shook his head from side to
side. "What a goddamn waste it would be, Liz. Makes my
heart break."

She was silent. A bluff, that was all. But how could she
know with a guy like Marino? "Okay," she said. "Go
ahead. Book me. Why don't you do that?"

"I intend to."

It was like the sound of a heavy metal door slamming.
She could hear it echo, rattling, in her mind.

"The jury's going to go for your guts, sweetheart. Such
a violent crime." He watched her, drumming his desk
with his fingertips. "Very nasty. They don't like that. An
open razor. No, they won't like that at all. . . ."

She wanted to challenge him again. She wanted to say:
Book me. But she didn't have the heart to say it a second
time.

"Tomorrow," he said. "Unless something turns up between now and then, I'll book you tomorrow."

"Unless what turns up?" she said.

"Oh . . ." He paused. He touched his moustache, stroking it lightly. "I don't know. A certain appointments
book, maybe."

"Hold it. Just hold it a moment."

"I mean," Marino said. "You're a paranoid murder
suspect. You're not expected to behave rationally, not
with your head on the chopping block. A certain appointments book might just *happen* to come your way."

"No—"

"Stir crazy. They tell me that's the worst thing that can
happen to a person in the slammer."

"Marino—are you asking me to get inside Elliott's
office and steal that goddamn book for you? Is that what
you're asking me?"

"I didn't say that, did I?"

"The hell you didn't—"

He sat down, looked at some papers again, straight-
ened them out.

She said, "There's a word for this, Marino. A nasty
word."

"Yeah?"

"Fucking blackmail."

"Me? Blackmail you? I'm a cop, lady. I don't break laws. I uphold them. It's my sworn duty."

"Like hell."

He started to write something, ignoring her. Without looking up, he said, "Tomorrow."

She hesitated a moment, then she went quickly to the door.

When she'd gone out he sat back smiling.

2

It was shortly after midday when she met Peter at a cafeteria on West Fifty-seventh Street. He was sitting in a far corner of the place, smothering a hamburger with ketchup. As she approached him he looked up smiling, and she thought: What an unlikely alliance this is. A hooker and a kid, sharing a common purpose. She slid into the seat facing him.

"You always use that much ketchup?" she asked.

"It takes the taste away," he said. "What happened?"

"With Marino?"

He nodded, biting into the hamburger. A slick of ketchup fell on to his plate.

"He's given me what you might call an ultimatum, kid."

"Like how?"

"You shouldn't talk with your mouth full."

"Yeah, I know."

"He wants me to get inside Elliott's office and take a look at his appointments book."

"How are you going to do that?"

Liz took a cigarette from her purse. "I had a bright idea. At least it seemed bright when I thought about it. It seemed even brighter still when I considered the alternative—the slammer."

"You want to tell me about it?"

She hesitated. "I don't think I like the idea, but I can't think of anything better. . . ."

Peter put down his half-eaten hamburger and leaned forward across the table to listen.

3

George Levy's office was located in a building on Forty-second Street. As he rode up in the elevator Elliott tried to suppress the nervousness he felt. It had been a restless night, moments of light sleep punctuated with thoughts of his wife, with thoughts of Bobbi too—the idea that somehow she'd been able to get inside the office when he was out. And once, when he'd dreamed, he imagined her standing over him with an open razor, her face grim, her words sounding as if they were spoken in an echo chamber: *Your time is coming too, Elliott. Make no mistake.* . . .

He got out of the elevator and followed the signs to Levy's office. The reception room was Naugahyde and rubber plants and piped Muzak; the girl behind the desk was attractive in a plastic way, as if Levy had selected her from a Sears catalogue—the kind of girl you might see modelling the latest in bikinis. He announced himself at the desk. The girl smiled, rose, and showed him into an inner office. Levy rose, his hand extended, Elliott shook it; the girl withdrew.

"I'm sorry I couldn't see you before," Levy said. "You know how it is—busy schedule, et cetera. Sit down."

Elliott sat, facing the desk. He gazed at George Levy a moment. He was a plump little man with a mass of unruly gray hair. He had the sort of expression that suggested he was forever scrutinizing, forever analyzing; it was a look under which Elliott felt distinctly uncomfortable. There was something else too, something Elliott felt only in a vague way—that Levy was familiar to him. Maybe they'd met at some convention, or at a symposium.

Levy smiled. "I'm at a loss to understand what it is you want to see me about, I'm afraid. I hope you can enlighten me."

"I think I can," Elliott said. "It concerns a former patient of mine, someone I understand you're treating now."

Levy glanced at his watch, then raised his face to look

at Elliott. There was an expression on Levy's face, an expression that might have been one of uncertainty, of bewilderment, but it passed quickly.

"I understand the need for confidentiality," Elliott said, smiling in a weak way. "But there are special circumstances involved here. . . ."

"It would help if you named the patient involved—"

"Bobbi—"

"Ah, yes, Bobbi." Levy took out his pipe and lit it, stuffing it from a cracked leather pouch. He spent several matches before he had the pipe lit.

"I have no doubt in my mind," Elliott said, "that she's dangerous."

"Dangerous?"

Elliott paused. "She's threatened to cause me trouble because I refused to approve a sex change operation."

"Why did you refuse?"

"It was my opinion—and it still is—that she isn't a true transsexual."

"Perhaps you can explain that to me, Dr. Elliott."

"A true transsexual has an unalterable belief that she is one sex trapped, so to speak, in the body of the other. In the case of Bobbi, however, she is not aware of her *other* self—and it was my diagnosis that she's really a dangerous schizophrenic personality. That her treatment should not involve a sex change operation but instead drug and behavioral therapy in a confined environment."

"Such as a mental institution?"

"Exactly."

Levy stared at him. Elliott looked away—why was the stare so damnably unnerving?

"What kind of trouble has she caused you?" Levy asked.

Elliott paused again. The edge, the darkness below, but how could he go on protecting Bobbi?

He said, "There have been telephone calls of a troublesome nature. If it were only that, of course, I don't think I should be so worried as I am. However . . ."

Levy looked at him questioningly.

"She also stole my razor from my office."

"Why?"

"Did you read about the woman who was slashed to death in an elevator?"

"The news was hard to miss—"

"The dead woman was a patient of mine, Dr. Levy—"

"And you think Bobbi killed her with your razor?"

"The conclusion is hard to avoid." Elliott cleared his throat, the roof of his mouth was dry. "And I have every reason to believe that she'll kill again. She said as much."

"You haven't informed the police?"

Elliott shook his head. "Not yet. I wanted to talk with her. I wanted to be absolutely sure it was her. But I can't locate her. So I came to you."

Levy was silent for a long time, knocking sparks from his pipe into an ashtray. "I'll talk with her," he said eventually. "If I concur with your prognosis, we'll get in touch with the police."

Elliott began to rise. "Please let me know what happens."

"Of course," Levy said. "Before you go, do you want to know why she came to see me in the first place?"

"I assume it was because she imagined you would approve her operation, after I'd refused—"

Levy got up from his chair, went to a cabinet, unlocked it. He took out a small casette and placed it inside a tape player.

"I want you to listen to this, Dr. Elliott. Since we both know the same patient, and the specific problems, I don't feel I'm breaking a confidence."

Elliott watched as Levy pushed the PLAY button.

There was a hissing sound, then he heard Bobbi's voice, interrupted only occasionally by a question from Levy.

"I went to a boarding school for a time. . . ."

"Did something specific happen there? Something you remember?"

"The games . . . I remember the games. . . . I wasn't very good at them. . . . But that isn't really what I remember most. Just this sense of being different. Being different from the other kids there. I felt alone. I felt miserably alone. I find it . . . hard to explain how bad I felt, how dark inside. . . ."

"What about the other kids?"

"They knew. They noticed. I know they noticed I was different."

Elliott closed his eyes, listening. That familiar voice. How cold it sounded.

"Tell me about the difference you felt?"

"What can I tell you about unhappiness?"

"Well, can you tell me about something that made you *happy?*"

A pause. A crackling sound, like paper being ripped.

"Once, when I went home during a vacation, I . . ."

Another pause.

"What did you do, Bobbi?"

"I put on my sister's clothes. I was found out."

"What happened then?"

"I was scolded. . . . But it didn't matter, you see. It didn't matter then. Because for the first time I understood who I was, I understood what I was, what I wanted to be. . . . And there was this thing between my legs, this cock, and I remember thinking how much I had to get rid of it. . . . I never stopped thinking about how badly I had to get rid of it."

"This idea persisted—"

"Persisted! I never stopped thinking about it, not once, not during all the time I was growing up . . . and when I started to go out in female clothes, I knew then I had to get the operation. . . . But Elliott, you see, Elliott wouldn't sign. He wouldn't let me do it. . . ."

Elliott leaned forward, his eyes still shut, listening intently.

"So that's when you tried it yourself?"

"I took a razor, right. I took this really sharp razor and I tried . . ."

Levy pushed the STOP button.

"She tried to hack off her genitals," he said.

Elliott said nothing.

"That's when she was sent to me."

"When was this? When did this happen?"

"About two months ago."

Elliott shook his said: "God. I didn't know she'd gone that far. I just didn't realize . . . ."

He looked at Levy. Levy was rubbing his chin, watching him as if he were blaming him for failing Bobbi.

"If you like, I'll try and talk with her this afternoon," Levy said. "I'll get back to you. Will you be in your office?"

Elliott nodded. He said, "Thanks for your time, Dr. Levy."

"I'll be in touch," Levy said.

4

It was just after three and raining violently when Marino picked up his two kids from school. They had expressions of incredulity, as if after a series of broken engagements and disappointments they had come to expect the worst—a telephoned excuse, a last-minute change of plans. It gave Marino a warm feeling not to let them down for once; it gave him a sense of belonging once again to a family unit—a unit he had come to realize, over the years, that was fragile at best. They clambered into the back of the car, dripping rainwater over his seats. What the hell, he didn't have the heart to point out this mess to them. He wasn't especially fond of basketball even but he liked the idea of the kids having a good time. He liked even more the prospect of getting out of the office for a while, out of that world of violence and mayhem, and back to something that was basically innocent.

As he drove through the heavy traffic, watching his windshield wipers whip back and forth across the glass, he glanced at the kids in his rearview mirror. "Cut the noise down, guys, huh? In this kind of crap weather, I really need to concentrate, you know?"

They smiled at him with the expressions of tolerance reserved by kids for their parents.

"Solved any crimes lately?" the younger one asked.

"Yeah, solve them every day," Marino said.

They were nudging each other in the backseat, like some private joke was going on.

"Hey, I'm good at my job, you guys. What do you think—I never catch a killer, huh?"

"I bet you catch them all the time," the younger one said.

The older one smirked and covered his mouth with the palm of his hand.

"What's the big joke?" Marino said.

They exchanged conspiratorial looks, then they started to laugh.

"I'll tell you something," Marino said. "It ain't the easiest thing in the world being a cop."

He looked again in the rearview mirror.

"Colombo always gets his man," the older kid said.

"Fairy tales," Marino said.

"Maybe. But he always traps the killer."

"Me and Colombo," Marino said. "All we've got in common is the raincoat."

"You brush your hair, though. Colombo doesn't."

"Listen. In my precinct, that guy wouldn't last a minute."

He pulled up at a stop sign. He was thinking all at once of Liz Blake. Put her out of your mind, he told himself. You owe yourself a couple of hours without pondering homicide. Don't you?

Liz stepped out of the phone booth. Peter was standing in the doorway of a store, watching her. She rushed across the sidewalk, the collar of her coat turned up, the wind blowing rain through her hair. When she reached the doorway she ran her fingers through her wet hair.

Peter looked at her questioningly.

"It's set," she said. "All systems go."

He shook his head; his expression was one of worry.

"I don't like the idea, really."

"Can you think of a better one?"

"No," he answered after a time.

Liz stared bleakly through the rain. "Hey, let's go get something to eat. We can pass some time that way."

"I'm not hungry," Peter said.

"Me neither."

They stood in silence, watching the rain, watching the city darken as night began to fall—the early dark dragged in its wake by the storm.

George Levy had a bad attack of indigestion, a feeling he usually only managed to alleviate with music. It was

presumably a psychosomatic thing, and Vivaldi's *Concer-*
to Grosso in B Minor always seemed to settle his stomach. There was a growling noise somewhere in the center
of his belly as he took the tape of Bobbi out of the casette
player and dropped in the Vivaldi. Then he sat down,
hands clasped across his stomach.

As he listened to the music, to the largo movement, he
thought about Bobbi, then about Elliott. And it occurred
to him that there was only thing to do, only one way
to clarify matters. He picked up his telephone, hesitated a
moment before punching out a number, then he dialled the
police.

5

Liz pushed the door open, stepped inside the lobby. The
reception room, which was to her right, was empty. She
entered, looked around, stared at the dust-covered typewriter on the desk, the magazines neatly piled on a table,
the sofas. Okay, she thought, you need to settle these
nerves. You're a troubled woman, don't forget. You've
got problems. Real problems. And they're urgent
ones. . . .

She sat down on one of the sofas, crossed her legs, lit a
cigarette. From outside she could hear a roar of thunder,
the wind sweeping the rain against the window. Her hand
shook as she raised the cigarette to her mouth. The
smoke tasted bitter against her tongue.

She heard a noise from the inner office, and then Elliott
was standing in the open doorway, smiling at her.

She stood up.

"Miss Blake?"

She nodded. She followed him into the inner office,
where he sat down behind his desk.

"Why don't you sit?" he said.

She moved towards the sofa. On the surface of his desk
there were a number of papers, books, copies of correspondence. The appointments book, she thought. How
was she supposed to get a look at the appointments book,
even if she could find the goddamn thing?

"It was good of you to see me at such short notice,"
she said.

"I happened to have a cancellation," he said. "Besides, when you told me about your experience on the telephone, how could I *not* see you?"

She gazed at him. Behind him, flashing against the window, there was a splitting arch of lightning in the darkened sky.

"It wasn't so much being a witness to a killing ..." She faltered now, wondering what to say next, wondering if he could see through her, see the playacting. "That was bad enough. But I've been having these nightmares since then. ..." Another sword of lightning. She blinked involuntarily.

"Tell me about the nightmares," he said.

"They're not pleasant. ..."

"I'm used to hearing about dreams," he said.

She closed her eyes. Okay, she thought. Make it up. Make it up real quick. "I'm in this room someplace. ... Look, it's hard for me to tell you."

"Pretend I'm not here," he said.

"Okay, I'll try. I'm in this room, and there's some kind of dinner party, only I don't know any of the guests. They're all strangers to me. I'm eating something, I don't know what, maybe some kind of shellfish. Anyhow, I feel something touching my ankle ... Somebody's hand."

"Somebody under the table?"

"Yeah, right. The hand starts to work up my leg. It's weird. Sitting at this dinner party with somebody touching me. ... The hand goes up, it just keeps going up. ..." She paused. Where was the fucking appointments book?

"Go on," Elliott said. "What happens next?"

"It's really grotesque. ... The hand goes right up under my skirt, see. Then it isn't a hand any longer, it's somebody's mouth. Somebody's mouth sucking me off. The terrible part about it all is that although I want to scream or just get up and go away, I'm beginning to enjoy myself. ... The mouth keeps on eating me under the table and I start to have this terrific orgasm. And while I'm having it, I have to go on pretending that nothing's happening. ..."

Elliott was silent a moment. "Why do you call it a bad dream? What makes it a nightmare?"

"It's a nightmare because it's out of the ordinary, everything's so twisted, especially after it changes—"

"How does it change?"

"I'm all alone in the room, maybe it's the same room, maybe it's not, I don't know— Anyhow, I'm all alone and these hands are lashing me to a table with rope, and the rope is really cutting into me, really painful, and then there's a whole succession of men fucking me, and every time it happens the pain gets worse until it's totally unbearable. . . ."

She paused. She stared at him. He was watching her with a strange intensity.

"Believe me, it's bad. And I'm an expert on bad."

"What makes you an expert on bad?"

"I should tell you up front—I'm a hooker. You name it, I've done it."

He was silent for a moment. Then, "You enjoy what you do?"

"Yeah. Sometimes. I like the idea that I can turn a guy on."

"Do you ever have sex where there's no money involved?" he asked.

"Do you ever give free consultations?"

"It's not exactly the same thing, is it?"

"I don't know. I don't see much difference."

Elliott smiled, leaning forward, picking up a paperweight and stroking it lightly.

Liz said, "It gives me a special pleasure, you know—I turn a guy on, I get a kind of a high that way."

She crossed her legs. She saw him glance at her thigh. She pretended not to notice. He let the paperweight fall from his fingers.

"Let's get back to the nightmares," he said. "Why do you think they're related to the fact you witnessed a killing?"

"You're the expert. You tell me—are they related?"

"It's hard to say. Sometimes the trauma . . ." He stopped, as if some thought had suddenly crossed his mind, a notion he didn't like. She watched him a moment. It occurred to her that perhaps the appointments book wasn't on his desk, that it was outside in the reception room, maybe stuck in the drawer of the desk out there. How the hell was she going to find out?

Your only weapon, kid, is your body.

There was a strangely distant look in his eye, like his mind was elsewhere now. She stretched her legs, showing more thigh, more pale flesh.

"Do I turn *you* on?"

She saw the question surprised him. He frowned, looking away from her. "Would it give you some pleasure to think you did?"

"Like I told you—a slight high. Anyhow, I'm more interested in the mature fatherly type. But maybe you don't find *me* interesting?"

"I didn't say that."

"Then why don't you do something about it?"

"Look, I'm a married man—"

"Most of my customers are," she said. She tried to see his expression, but he had his face still turned to the side. "And some of them have been married *doctors.*"

He faced her now. A flash of lightning, like a brilliant rocket sent up in some celebration, lit his features. But she wasn't sure what she saw there—anger? concern? Maybe it was neither of these things, maybe it was interest. He stood up twisting his hands together, cracking the knuckles. She thought: The reception room. The desk. If she could only get a chance to look.

But how?

"Look, aren't we straying somewhat from the point?" he said.

"I like your accent. It's cute," she said. *Cute,* how she hated that particular word.

"It's very kind of you to say so, I'm sure—"

"But I mean it." She got up from the sofa and walked towards him. She placed her hands against his shoulders. Gently, he moved her away.

"Look, you came here because of certain psychological problems . . ."

"Yeah, but maybe something a little more basic than psychiatry could solve them, Doc—"

"I hardly think so."

She stared at him. Something cold in the eyes, something

of steel, as if he were struggling with desire, as if he were afraid of it rising up inside him.

He became patient, smiling at her in a rather sad way. He said, "I have a certain code of conduct in my profession. I don't become involved sexually with my patients—"

"Am I a patient?"

"I'm beginning to wonder if I need you as a patient," he said.

She leaned closer to him. Another flare of lightning flooded the room, rampant unfettered electricity. His desk lamp flickered momentarily.

"I could be *more* than just a patient. . . ."

He moved his face to the side. She saw then the glistening film of sweat that lay on the surface of his forehead and she thought: I'm reaching him. I'm getting to him.

She put her hand up, turned his face around towards her, kissed him full on the mouth—a strange kiss, a kiss of ice, a lack of response. Once again, he pushed her gently away.

"I told you—"

"I think you're full of shit. I think you'd like nothing better than to screw me. You know that? I think you'd love to fuck me right now, wouldn't you? You'd love to take my clothes off real slow. Feel my tits. Or maybe you'd like me to strip and go down on you. I'm pretty good at that, Doc. I give terrific head."

"No," he said. "I don't want to discuss—"

"I know a few exotic tricks as well," she said. "Things your wife never dreamed about, I bet. I could drive you out of your fucking mind."

She laid the palm of her hand against his chest, undoing a button, wanting to press her fingers to his flesh, but he drew away, stepped back, his face now drenched in perspiration.

"You're hard, aren't you? I can see. Your cock is hard. You're ready for me, aren't you?"

"No!"

"Don't fuck around with me, Doc. Don't play any smartass games."

She unbuttoned her blouse and let if fall to the floor.

He watched her. He wants me, she thought. He wants me now.

She stepped out of her skirt and stood in front of him in her bra and pants, smiling. With her hands on her hips she said, "Well? You approve?"

"Please . . ."

"Please what?"

He went back behind his desk, as if there he might find some kind of safety.

"For God's sake, put your clothes on," he said. *"Please."*

"I'm getting to you, is that it? You like what you see? Huh?"

He closed his eyes, his hands pressed against the surface of the desk, and he swayed slightly. There was a moment, just a fraction of time, when she felt a strange sense of pity for him, an indefinable sorrow. Maybe he wants to be faithful to his wife. Maybe that's it, and maybe what I'm doing is all wrong.

But then she remembered the dying woman in the elevator, she remembered the blonde with the hideous black glasses, and her sorrow disintegrated. He's protecting a killer. I'm supposed to feel bad on his account?

"I got it," she said. "You're shy. Is that it?"

With his eyes shut, he nodded his head. He spoke and his voice was hoarse. "Yes. I'm shy."

"You're shy and I'm understanding. So I'll give you a break."

He opened his eyes and looked at her curiously.

"I'll wait in the other room. I'll come back in a few minutes and if your clothes aren't lying beside mine on the floor, we'll forget the whole deal. Okay?"

For a second she thought he was going to pick up her discarded clothing and throw it at her, because what flashed across his face was a confused look of anger and distaste. She turned, opened the door, stepped inside the reception room. She closed the door behind her.

She went to the desk.

She opened a drawer.

Papers, paper clips, a shrivelled apple. Typewriter cartridges, a box of Kleenex, a hair ribbon. Some windowed envelopes, invoices.

Where is the goddamn appointments book?
Where?

Peter couldn't feel the numbing rain any more. His clothes were stuck to his body, but he was beyond feeling the chill. He didn't like the idea of Liz being in there on her own, but it had been her idea. *I get the appointment book, the names, and I save my ass with our old pal Marino.*

He had tried to think of a better way. But nothing came, no idea, no plan. And Liz had said, *You stay out of this, okay? I don't want you involved in the rest of it.*

How could he have done that, Christ?

He'd gone home, found his binoculars; sneaking in and out of the apartment, noticing the open door of his mother's bedroom and the sight of Mike lying on top of the bed, fully dressed, asleep. A half-empty scotch bottle sat on the bedside table. Poor goddamn Mike; he has to drink his grief away.

Now, across the street from Elliott's office, he saw Liz take her clothes off. He couldn't figure it for a moment, thinking only that she had a real terrific body, like the kind he sometimes sneaked a look at it in *Playboy* or *Gallery*. But what the hell was she doing? He wiped smears of rain from the lenses of the binoculars. Liz had gone out of the room and now he couldn't see her any more, but he could see Elliott, he could see Elliott standing in the middle of his office, motionless, not doing anything, just standing there like he was waiting for something to happen. Then he moved, opening a closet door.

Opening a closet door and—

But rain streamed in oleaginous streaks across the lenses and he had to wipe them dry again. Then he trained the glasses on the window once more, watching the figure of Elliott sliced by the open slats of the blinds.

What the hell is he doing?

What is he doing in that closet?

He screwed his eyes up, trying hard to see. Trying so hard he didn't notice a dark car draw up a little way down the block and a blonde woman step out.

Liz found the appointments book in the bottom drawer of the desk. Yesterday, she thought. Peter took the photographs yesterday. Okay, find the names, find the names, and one of those names belongs to the killer. She flipped the pages hastily, suddenly cold in the room, trembling as she turned the pages over. Her mind went blank abruptly. What the hell was yesterday's date? Jesus Christ. Can't think. What day was it? Wednesday? Thursday? She kept flipping, expecting at any moment the door to the inner office to be opened from inside, expecting to turn and see Elliott standing there and watching her.

I have to kill her. I have no choice. She has to die. She should have died before.

Peter slung the binoculars over his shoulder, the strap dangling loosely. He felt a strange uneasiness. Liz had gone out of the room and she hadn't returned. Why? Where was she? What was keeping her? *Maybe she's hurt. Maybe she needs help.* He hesitated only a moment longer, then moved across the street.

Elliott had laid his clothes down beside Liz's. He had folded them neatly. Then he'd opened the closet and stared at the hangers inside. He listened to her in the reception room. She was doing something, turning pages, maybe passing time by reading a magazine. He inclined his head, listening, then he reached inside the closet.

She's in there. She has to die. Her death is necessary. This time I won't fail. The pearl-handled razor will do it this time.

Peter reached the door.
Too late.
A fraction too late.
He felt a hand clamped around his mouth from behind and, trying to twist, to bite, saw a tall blonde woman from the corner of his eye. She swung him around, her palm still pressed against his lips; he felt a roar of blood in his head, a rush of his pulses, a sense of darkness falling over him. The blonde drew him towards the door

and pushed it open quietly. He was aware of being in a
lobby now. It was hard to breath, hard to draw air, so
tight was her hand against his mouth. Please, he thought.
Please. I don't need to die.

She pushed the door softly shut behind her, gripping
him harder as he tried to struggle.

Liz found the page, looked down the list of names.
There were only a half dozen or so: and one of them was
the killer. All she had to do was tear the page from the
book, get it to Marino, and he could do the rest. She
began to rip it quietly from the binding. As she did so, the
door of the inner office opened.

She pulled her hand away from the book, thinking of
something to say, thinking of how she could pass her
curiosity off as a joke.

*Just nosey, ha ha. Never could resist prying. Some
people are like that, Doc, and I guess I'm one of them, ha
ha—*

She turned, trying not to look guilty.

She turned, expecting to see Elliott come out of the
inner office.

Expecting to see . . .

The razor rose in the air, gleaming, seeming to hang
there like time had ceased, like all the clocks of the world
had stopped. She watched it, saw the brilliant mirror of
the metal blade as it was suspended in the air, saw the
blonde hair curiously askew on the skull, saw the dress,
the hairless legs under the dress, the bare feet, the strange
misshapen slash of lipstick across the mouth.

Oh dear Christ—

She swung her head to the side as the razor came down.
She struck her spine against the corner of the desk,
moaned in pain, and then tried to crawl away from the
descent of the razor. It swung so close to the side of her
neck that she could hear its dreadful whisper. She rolled
over, still moaning, seeing the bare feet come forward;
and then, looking up, seeing the light of hatred and
madness in the eyes, and the razor came swinging down
again, catching the strap of her bra and slicing it, paring
the surface of her flesh.

You have to die. Bobbi has to kill you. You saw too much.

She tried to rise up, hauling herself against the edge of
the desk. She heard the feet brushing the rug behind her.
Scream, scream, scream—goddamnit, why can't you
fucking scream? She felt a hand grab the elastic of her
pants, tugging at it, and she pulled herself free as the
flimsy material ripped. She moved around the side of the
desk, watching the razor again, watching as it created a
blinding arc on its downswing, as it whistled just past her
wrist and slashed the wooden edge of the desk, creating a
flying splinter. Fight, fight, find something to fight with,
anything, any weapon you can grab, anything. She stared
at the face as it came closer to her and the razor rose
again—that deranged face, the wild blonde hair, the lipstick that looked like a bloodstain. The razor rose and
fell, slashing close to her arm, so close she could feel a
wave of air parting. She twisted away, reaching for a
potted fern that stood on a table beside the desk, lifting
the plant up and throwing it haphazardly at the blonde,
seeing it strike the woman's shoulder in an explosion of
dirt and leaf. The blonde moaned, rubbed her shoulder,
momentarily let the hand that held the razor fall to her
side. Liz rushed round the side of the desk, heading for
the door—but too slow, too goddamn slow, because the
blonde stuck a leg out and tripped her and she fell
forward, rolling on her back, staring up as the razor came
swinging downward again. It missed the side of her neck,
striking the rug beneath her, slicing the pile of the rug
viciously. Liz tried to rise but the blonde pressed her knee
directly into her stomach, pinning her to the rug, raising
the blade again. Something. *Anything.* She twisted to the
side, raising her face, sinking her teeth into the blonde's
thigh, hearing the sound of the woman's pain. The face—
the face of pain and hatred, she had to get away from
that face as much as the razor, but even as she turned
over and began to crawl closer to the door she could hear
the woman's heavy breathing, the breathing of labor; she
could feel the heat of it upon her bare spine and she
knew, she knew without looking, that the razor was going

up in the air again, rising, rising only to fall, and this time when it fell it would slip through the back of her neck, through thin veins, flimsy muscles, through the surfaces of bone and deep into the hollow of the nape. She opened her mouth to scream, conscious of herself clawing at the tuft of the rug, aware of that terrible blade flashing through the air, aware even before it happened of her own blood rushing through the opening in her neck, her life bleeding out of her, red turning to darkness, and darkness a place beyond pain.

No!

She twisted again, tried to turn away, but the blonde was straddling her; she was too strong, too hard to fight, holding her against the rug with one hand while the other raised the blade for its final descent.

You die like this—bleeding—your last sight that of the lipsticked mouth twisted and open, the hair unruly and strange, the eyes bright with insanity, you die like this, dear Christ, watching the falling blade seek an artery—

You don't look.

Close your eyes.

There was a sudden noise, something she couldn't comprehend at first. There was no pain, no piercing of her throat, no blood, no sense of dying. She heard Peter's voice, but it was like a dream voice floating out of an unlit place. She felt dizzy, rolling her head backwards, seeing Peter standing over her, seeing a woman crossing the room with a pistol in her hand, seeing the woman— her blonde hair made shapeless by rain—stand over Elliott, who was clutching his shoulder and groaning in pain.

Liz closed her eyes.

The scream died somewhere in her lungs and all she was conscious of was Elliott's moaning, of his blonde wig lying some feet from where he lay—an absurd thing now, shapeless, useless, reminiscent of some extinct grotesque bird.

Peter was bending over her.

"You okay?"

She nodded.

"Just take it easy." He covered her with his wet jacket

and she shivered. All she could think to do was laugh, but the laughter, like the scream before it, wouldn't come.

"It's okay," Peter was saying. "It's over."

It's okay, she thought. It's over.

Over.

EIGHT

1

"I apologize for the coffee," Marino was saying. "I know it's pretty foul. Department funds don't run to a decent brand."

Liz stared at him across the desk. "I think you want to apologize for more than the goddamn coffee, Marino."

He waved a hand in an indeterminate gesture. "Okay. So I'm sorry. I said it."

"Sorry? Jesus Christ, Marino, I almost got myself killed!"

He looked at her as if he wanted to say, *These things happen.*

Liz raised her coffee, sipped, made a face. "I need a cigarette. Anybody got one?"

Marino pushed a pack across his desk.

"You don't have anything with a filter?" Liz asked.

"Once a Camel smoker, always a Camel smoker."

Liz lit the cigarette and coughed. She stared at the black window, startled a little when a broken flash of lightning slashed the sky over the city. She closed her eyes a moment. When she opened them again she saw Marino was smiling. How can that sonofabitch just sit there and *smile,* for God's sake?

She took another drag of the cigarette, trying to still the shaking of her hand, conscious of Marino staring at it. She looked away from the cop a moment, gazing at the face of the tall blonde woman who had shot Elliott. Seated at the other end of the desk was a short plump man who had been introduced as Dr. Levy. She had the odd feeling that they were gathered together for a séance, that at any moment a Ouija board would be dragged out of Marino's desk and an attempt made to contact the spirit world. She wanted to laugh.

Marino indicated the blonde woman. "This is Betty Luce. She's one of our best young policewomen."

Liz looked at the woman for a moment. "I ought to thank you," she said. "The funny thing is, I don't feel very much like thanking anybody right now."

"I had Betty Luce follow you, Liz," Marino said. He yawned, but didn't bother to cover it with his hand. Liz could see his upper metal fillings shining in a moist way. "She informed me that she lost you in the vicinity of Columbus Circle."

Liz shook her head. "So when I told you I was damn near killed in the subway you thought I wasn't playing with a full deck, is that it?"

"Something like that," Marino said. "How the hell was I supposed to know there was another blonde following you?"

"So you thought—well, here's a chick with a hyperactive imagination, is that it?"

Marino shrugged, sipped some more coffee. He was smiling again. Christ, she thought: *He's all smiles tonight*. The bastard, the ruthless bastard. His telephone rang, he picked it up, addressed a few terse words to somebody called Mary, then he hung up. "The wife," he explained. "She thinks I keep stinking hours. Maybe she's right."

Liz put down her cardboard container of coffee, then stubbed her cigarette out. Marino sighed, doodled something on his desk blotter, then wearily dropped his ballpoint pen.

"What the hell is wrong with that guy Elliott anyway?" Liz asked.

Dr. Levy, thumbs tucked inside the pockets of his vest, became suddenly animated. "It's both simple and complicated," he said.

"Just give me the simple," she said.

"In a proverbial nutshell, he was a transsexual about to make the final step. But his male side wouldn't allow it."

Marino looked bored. He began to pick his teeth.

"Explain a little more," Liz said.

Levy took an unlit pipe from his pocket and tapped it on the desk, scattering ashes that Marino regarded with disapproval.

"See if this makes sense to you," he said.

He had a patronizing manner that Liz found irritating.

"I'll try to get my little brain to work it over," she said.

The doctor either didn't catch her sarcasm or chose instead to ignore it. "Two distinct personalities. Bobbi on the one hand, Elliott on the other. Bobbi came to me for my approval for a sex change operation. I thought she—he—was unstable. A schizophrenic with a male personality within her. Make sense so far?"

Liz nodded. She felt a sudden wave of fatigue. Her eyelids were becoming heavy.

"Elliott came to see me. That was the first time I'd seen Bobbi's male self. And it was perfectly clear to me that he had no idea Bobbi existed inside him. Both selves, if you like, were unaware of each other. When Elliott told me he thought Bobbi had killed Kate Myers, he was confessing, so to speak, that he himself had killed her. It was then that I tried to get in touch with Detective Marino."

Liz stared at Marino angrily. "You *knew?* You knew this? And you let me go to that office anyhow? You really take the goddamn cake, Marino, you know that?"

"Hold, hold," Marino said. "I happened to be at a ball game with my kids. By the time Dr. Levy finally got in touch with me, you'd already gone to the office. So I dispatched Betty Luce. You can thank whatever good fortune smiles on you that I did send her—"

Liz slumped back in her chair. "Yeah. I'll pray tonight."

There was silence in the room for a moment.

"Why was Kate Myers killed anyhow?" Liz asked.

Levy opened an old-fashioned watch, clicking the lid back, checking the time. "Primarily because Bobbi wanted to hurt Elliott for what she perceived as his refusal to allow the sex change. A secondary reason, of course, is that Elliott found himself aroused by the poor woman—and the erection of his penis reminded Bobbi of the existence of a male self, of an unwanted organ."

Liz stared at Marino, who was sitting back with his

eyes closed, looking bored. The toothpick dangled from his lower lip.

"Which leaves me with one last question, Marino. If you're still awake, that is."

The cop lazily opened his eyes. "Shoot."

"How did Bobbi, Elliott, whoever the hell he is, get my address? I mean, how come she was waiting for me outside my apartment building?"

Marino didn't move for a moment. Then he opened a drawer in his desk and took out a folder, which he passed to Liz. "Your history, Liz. Your record sheet."

"I don't get it," she said.

"The night of the killing I interviewed him here in this office. Somewhat carelessly, I left your folder on my desk. I guess he looked. I guess he saw your name and address there."

"Simple, huh? And there I was imagining he was clairvoyant."

Liz sat back in silence. "You know, Marino, you could have had me killed. Twice over."

"Yeah, but I didn't."

Liz got to her feet. A weakness now, a failure of bone and muscle, a yielding of volition. She placed her hands on the surface of Marino's desk and leaned forward towards him.

"Tell me something, Marino."

"Anything you like."

"Did you really ever think I killed Kate Myers?"

A mysterious expression crossed his face. "I like to keep that kind of speculation to myself, Liz. Call it a trade secret."

She sighed and walked to the door.

"Is it safe for me to go back to my apartment now?"

"Elliott is locked away. We can only hope somebody lost the key," Marino said. "But the least I can do for you, Liz, is have a car take you home."

"That would be small thanks, Lieutenant. Very small thanks."

"It's better than nothing."

2

She slept a dead sleep, bottomless, dreamless, the kind of sleep in which you surrender yourself to darkness, in which the darkness is a magnificent comfort. When she woke, sun slicing through the parted drapes, she felt refreshed. She made some coffee, smoked a cigarette, then looked up Peter's telephone number in the directory. He answered almost at once, as if he'd been waiting for her call.

She explained, in an abbreviated way, what she'd learned about Elliott, hoping the kid wouldn't ask the kind of questions she couldn't answer. But he did anyhow. That restless curious mind, she thought. It moved around like a gnat in a bottle. Like a firefly.

"I don't get it—I mean, why would a guy want to be a woman?"

"Listen," she said. "Being a woman isn't such a bad deal."

"Well, I wouldn't want to be one."

"Elliott did. Or a part of him anyhow."

"So how does somebody like that go about it?"

"Hormones, I think."

He was quiet a moment. "I read about hormones. They're produced by living cells that circulate through the body fluids—"

"Yeah, I'm sure you're right, kid."

"So what effect would hormones have on a nut like Elliott?"

"Well . . . they make your beard stop growing. Your skin gets softer. After a while you start to develop breasts."

"Sounds sick."

"Then the next step is the sex change operation. They slice your penis. . . ."

"That makes me feel funny. I feel like I want to cross my legs."

"You want me to go on?"

"Sure."

"Okay. After all the male genitalia is surgically removed, an artificial vagina is constructed."

Peter was quiet for a moment. "I thought transsexuals were just like fags."

"No. It's not like that. They don't want to be men going to bed with other men, Peter. They want to be *women* going to bed with men."

"I think I've heard enough," Peter said. "What's going to happen to Elliott?"

"He's been committed. I doubt if he'll ever be considered sane enough to stand trial. Which is a relief, since it means I won't have to be the star witness."

"I hope he's locked away for life," Peter said.

"Me too." She paused. She searched for a cigarette and found only a crumpled empty pack. "Say, I'm going to miss having you around. What about getting together next week some time for lunch, huh?"

"I'd like that. I really would."

"Okay, kid. I'll give you a call."

"You promise?"

"I never break a promise."

She hung up. She sat at the kitchen table, thinking about the kid, thinking how for a short period of time their lives had become interwoven. And then her telephone was ringing.

It was Max.

"I'm not sure what to do with you, Liz. You keep promising to bring me some cash, remember? So far, sweet zero."

"I'm on my way, Max."

"Can I quote you on that?"

"Girl Scout's honor, sweetheart. I'll see you in about an hour."

"Why do I put up with you, huh?"

"Because secretly you have this burning passion for me, right?"

"How did you guess?"

"I see the way you look at me."

"Ah, Christ, I always knew I wore my goddamn heart on my sleeve."

"One hour," she said.

"One hour. It's going to seem like an eternity."

She laughed, putting the receiver down.

She walked to the window, staring down into the sunlit

street, watching the flow of traffic, thinking of a nightmare past, a bad dream ended. It was as if some black
weight had been lifted from her, some terrible pressure
alleviated.

Some days, she thought, you can feel good.

3

Darkness. Cold. Like floating in a tank of colorless water.
Shivering. Eyes open. A dark room. A pinprick of light
someplace. The inside of a camera. And the dreams. The
dreams of pain.

That small light.

What was it?

What was that tiny glow of light?

The shoulder ached.

Why did it ache like that?

She couldn't remember. She couldn't remember her
name.

Anything.

Try. Try to bring it back somehow.

You shouldn't wear Cecilia's clothes....

She stirred, turning her head, concentrating on that
light.

A shadow moved. The light was obscured. The shadow
moved again.

Cecilia's clothes ...

Anne.

*I can only put up with this to a small degree, Robert.
... I can't go on pandering to your tastes.... This isn't a
marriage any more, this is a travesty.... Do you know
how it makes me feel? Do you know how it demeans
me to see you dressed like that?*

You're sick.

Sick and perverted.

Anne, Robert. What did those names mean? Why were
there these disconnected echoes?

I knew two people once, Anne and Robert, and somehow they didn't live happily ever after, something went
wrong.... Something just went wrong.

The light. That light. The outline of somebody's head
moving against the light.

My name.

My name . . .

She sat upright, staring through the dark.

Bobbi!

I am Bobbi.

But . . .

Somebody out there, somebody out there beyond this dark room, doesn't believe I'm Bobbi.

Drugs. They must have been shooting me with drugs.

Limbs weak. Pain.

You're not happy here, are you Bobbi?

No, you don't want to be in this place, do you?

You want to be somewhere else.

Go. Go someplace else.

She watched the shadow move against the light. Then there were footsteps, heels clicking over the hardwood floor. A chemical smell. Something antiseptic. Something like that.

A hospital?

What are you doing in a hospital, Bobbi?

Get away from here. Find a way out.

Click, click, click, click.

Heels.

Somebody moving across the floor.

A dark outline passing the bed. Pausing. The sound of soft breathing, a scent of some kind, a chemical scent.

You are not happy here Bobbi; you are not happy in this place because there is something else you must do, someplace else you must go to.

Try and remember.

A girl.

Pretty.

You are a boy, Robert. Don't you understand? Boys do the things boys do. Next time you take anything of Cecilia's I'll punish you most severely.

The shadow hovered in the dark. Barely visible.

A metallic sound. Like what? Keys?

Why have they locked you here Bobbi?

Are you a prisoner?

A pencil-thin flashlight.

She closed her eyes. She heard the faint *whish* of liquid

being ejected from a hypodermic. A hand fell on her arm.
A hand raised her arm upwards.

But you aren't happy here Bobbi.

The touch of a needle. Soft breathing. A baby's breathing.

Quickly now.

It has to be done quickly.

Before the chance goes. Before the opportunity evapo-
rates.

The throat is soft. Very soft. The throat yields under
the tips of fingers. Yields, gives.

You hear something soft fall to the floor.

Something drop.

A slight moan, a slight gasping sound.

And then silence and the sight of the thin lamplight
somewhere in the distance.

Rise up. Rise up Bobbi.

Forget the pain and rise.

Forget how much it hurts.

4

The nurse in the white uniform and white headdress
climbed the subway steps to the street. The night air was
cold, but she seemed not to feel it. She paused to ex-
change a word with a news vendor outside the station,
glancing as she did so at the headline of a paper. It had
something to do with a crisis in the Middle East. She
barely noticed it. A little way down the page there was a
photograph of a man—it seemed familiar to her in some
way, but she knew it couldn't be. She read a part of the
headline, seeing only the first few words PSYCHIA-
TRIST ARRES—and then, shrugging, shaking her head
as if the state of the world appalled her, she crossed the
street.

She went inside an apartment building.

She pressed the button for the elevator.

When the car came she stepped inside. The car rose,
shuddering, slowly. She closed her eyes. It was strange,
she thought, how she felt a curious sense of peace. The
elevator came to a stop. She got out, walking along the

corridor. It was the sixth floor. For a moment, a passing
fragment of time, she forgot why she was here, forgot
what she'd come here for, forgot the number of the
apartment she wanted.

She paused. It would come back to her.

Apartment . . . what?

Ah, she remembered. Sixty-three.

She continued along the corridor, stopped outside the
door of sixty-three, and gazed a moment at the small
peephole set in the wood. She hesitated, raised her hand,
then knocked very lightly on the panel.

She waited.

From inside she could hear a movement, the sound of
someone coming.

Liz put her tube of lipstick down on the dressing table,
picked up her watch, checked the time. She had an
appointment at nine; unless she hurried, she was going to
be late. When she heard the door she stared at herself in
the mirror, puckered her lips, and then went across the
living room. In the distance somewhere she could hear the
sound of a siren slashing through the night.

At the front door she paused, pressing her eye to the
peephole.

A nurse, she thought. What the hell was a nurse doing
out there?

Without opening the door, she said, "Yeah? What is
it?"

"I don't like to trouble you," the woman said. "I'm
simply collecting for a good cause. . . ."

"Oh, yeah, sure."

Liz opened the door, sliding the chain.

The nurse stepped inside.

Liz smiled, turned to find her purse, and then glanced
around to look at the nurse.

"I think I've got a couple of dollars somewhere—will
that be enough?" she asked. She picked up the purse, saw
the nurse's reflection in the mirror in front of her, saw
the headdress being thrown back, saw the shaved skull and
the empty grin, saw the white-smocked figure advance
towards her.

A dream, Liz thought.

A bad dream.

In a moment she would wake.

Any moment now, she would open her eyes and the dream would be over.

But it hadn't yet begun.

ABOUT THE AUTHORS

BRIAN DE PALMA, world-renowned thriller director, has been dubbed "The Prince of Terror" by the press. Raised in Philadelphia, he studied Physics at Columbia University. While taking an M.A. at Sarah Lawrence College, Mr. De Palma shot his first successful film, an award-winning short. He supported himself by making documentaries for the Treasury Department and the NAACP and then made his first feature film, *The Wedding Party*, starring two unknowns, Robert De Niro and Jill Clayburgh. Mr. De Palma's first major success with a mass audience came with *Obsession*, followed by the back-to-back box office hits, *Carrie* and *The Fury*. His newest release, *Dressed to Kill*, promises to continue this pattern. Brian De Palma is married to actress Nancy Allen, whom he met when she read for a part in *Carrie*. Though they are frequently on the West Coast, the De Palmas maintain their permanent residence in New York City where they enjoy quiet evenings at home, dinner with friends and, of course, movies of all kinds—but very rarely thrillers.

CAMPBELL BLACK was born in Glasgow, Scotland and educated at the University of Sussex, where he received an Honours Degree in Philosophy. His novel, *The Punctual Rape*, won the Scottish Arts Council Award in 1970. He has written many other novels, including *Brainfire*. Mr. Black is presently living in Tempe, Arizona with his wife and three sons.

Bantam Book Catalog

Here's your up-to-the-minute listing of over 1,400 titles by your favorite authors.

This illustrated, large format catalog gives a description of each title. For your convenience, it is divided into categories in fiction and non-fiction—gothics, science fiction, westerns, mysteries, cookbooks, mysticism and occult, biographies, history, family living, health, psychology, art.

So don't delay—take advantage of this special opportunity to increase your reading pleasure.

Just send us your name and address and 50¢ (to help defray postage and handling costs).